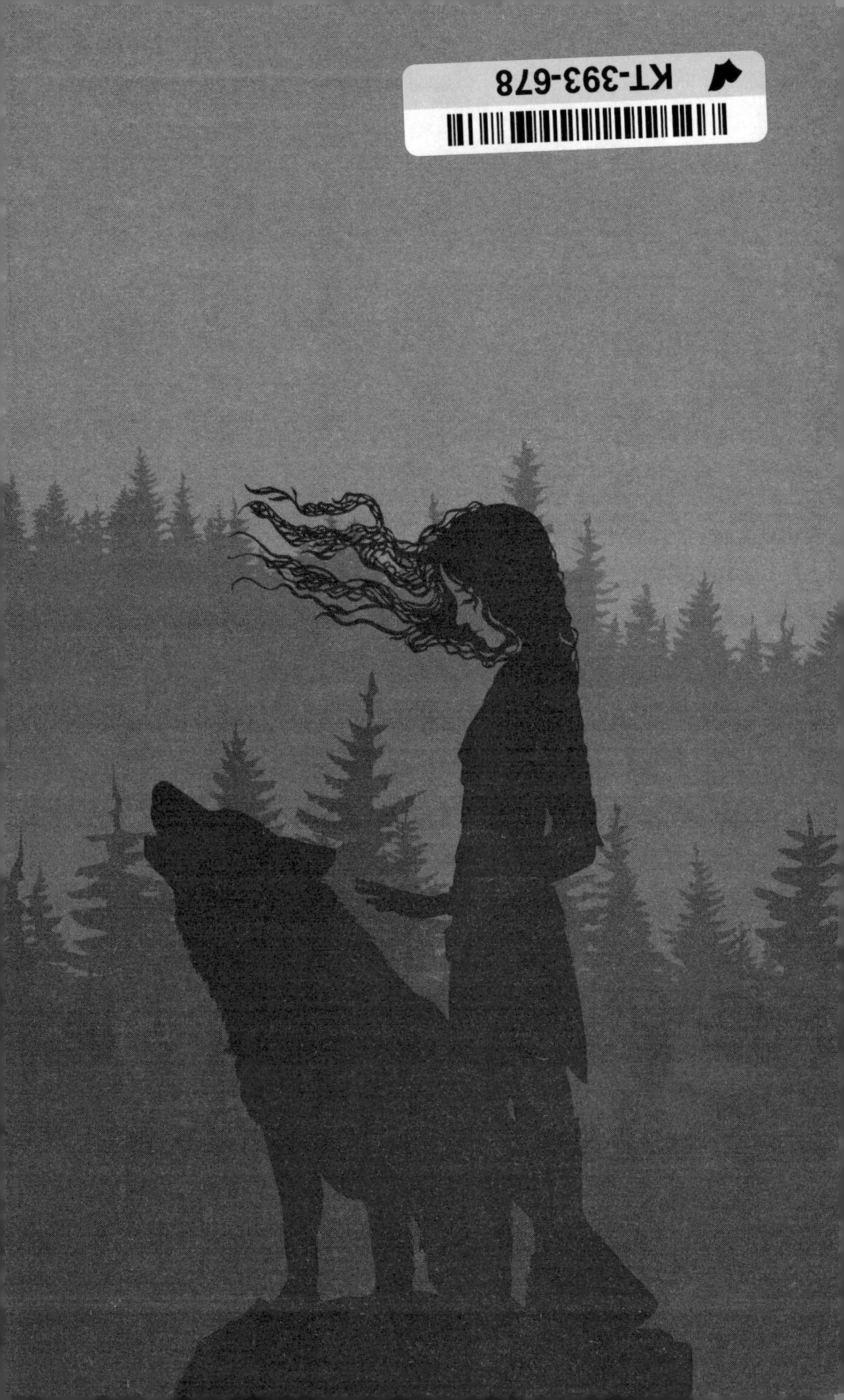

For Nancy Eveline, a friend to all animals – KH

For my mum, Patricia – CC

STRIPES PUBLISHING
An imprint of Little Tiger Press
1 The Coda Centre, 189 Munster Road,
London SW6 6AW

A paperback original
First published in Great Britain in 2015
Text copyright © Kris Humphrey, 2015
Illustration copyright © Chellie Carroll, 2015
Cover images courtesy of www.shutterstock.co.uk

ISBN: 978-1-84715-596-2

A WHISPER OF WOLVES

Kris Humphrey

Illustrated by Chellie Carroll

Stripes

THE WESTERN
OCEAN

CATCHWOOD

THE GREAT
FOREST

MERIDAR

INLAND SEA

THE ENDLESS
PLAIN

THE RIFTLANDS

CHAPTER 1

Alice hurried through the narrow streets of Catchwood. Today was market day and the village was packed with traders from all over the mountainside; boots, hooves and cart wheels rumbled across the hard-packed mud. Alice clutched a heavy wicker basket and the jars and pots within clanked together as she wove through the market-day traffic.

She stepped aside to allow a line of mules to pass and, as she did so, she noticed an elderly man sitting beside her in the doorway of a low-ceilinged cottage, carving a chunk of wood. Alice nodded at him politely as she waited, but the man simply narrowed his eyes, casting her a look of unconcealed suspicion.

Alice turned back to the street, her cheeks

burning with embarrassment and anger. She should have grown used to this by now, but her visits to the village remained as uncomfortable as ever. She tried to believe what Moraine, her mentor, had told her: that although the villagers feared her now, they would come, in time, to respect her as their Whisperer. But how long would she have to wait? She was twelve years old now and had been living here, apprenticed to Moraine, since she was old enough to walk.

She stared down at her boots and the mud stains on her long, patterned skirt – the one Moraine always insisted she wore into the village. When the last of the mules had gone by, Alice left the old man to his work, wishing she were back in the forest already.

The market square was a chaos of stalls and wagons. There were so many people – and so many animals, pulling carts or tethered to the posts and fences around the edges of the square. Colourful awnings flapped in the breeze and the stallholders bellowed their prices, vying for the custom of the crowds. Above it all stood the festival tree: a solitary pine that rose up, ancient and proud. And above the tree, the autumn sky raced with clouds.

Despite the cries of the sellers, with their ferocious bustle and salesmanship, one fact could not be hidden – most of the stalls were pitifully empty. There was simply not enough food to fill the market.

It had been a hard summer on the mountain. Edible plants had grown sparse, the streams and rivers were all but empty of fish, and those who hunted rabbit and deer were forced to travel further than ever before. In fact, the village's main hunting party had set out four days ago and not yet returned. This was the first time in years that they had missed a market day and people were beginning to talk.

Alice edged through the crowd. She hefted the wicker basket and aimed for Sal's grain stall, her first call of the day. The shadow of the festival tree slid over her and with it, like an all-powerful tide, came the smells and sounds of the traders. Alice was shoved aside by people carrying huge sacks and crates; elbows jabbed at her from every angle. It was simply the bustle of market day – she knew this – but every nudge and push made her feel even less welcome in the village than she already did.

These errands were vital to Alice's training as a healer, but Alice knew there was more to being a Whisperer than quietly producing medicines for the villagers. There had been a time when the Whisperers were respected, and even obeyed, throughout the kingdom. Under the leadership of Queen Amina they had protected Meridina from the Narlaw and banished the demon armies back to the Darklands. Nowadays any mention of the Narlaw was greeted with a condescending shake of the head. They were little more than monsters from the history books, used for scaring children into doing their chores.

Alice wished that the demons were just ancient history, but she knew better than that. The missing hunters and the changes in the forest were small things, coincidences perhaps, but Alice felt a growing fear that something sinister was behind it all – and she knew Storm and the other wolves shared her suspicions.

She felt a pang of loneliness at the thought of Storm. But she could only ever enter the village alone. The people of Catchwood didn't understand her bond with Storm, and a fully grown wolf was not a welcome guest in any village.

She arrived at the grain stall and made her way to the front. The goods on display were meagre: half a dozen loaves, a stack of wheat-flour parcels, some salt and a single coil of dry red sausage. There would normally be four or five times as much, and an extra table of wheat and barley sacks in reserve behind the stall.

Alice waited her turn, listening in as Sal finished her conversation with another customer.

"They've been gone four days now..." said the boy. He was about Alice's age, but his face was drawn with worry. He wore the short leather apron of an apprentice blacksmith or carpenter.

"Don't you fret, Owen lad," said Sal. "I'm sure they've just gone further out, looking for a better hunting ground."

"Four days, though," said Owen. "Something has to be wrong. Dad's never been away so long before."

Sal smiled sympathetically and the boy glanced sideways at Alice as he turned to leave.

Alice met his gaze silently. Perhaps he recognized a similar, troubled expression on Alice's face because he nodded to her solemnly before he turned and vanished into the crowds.

"The usual, is it?" Sal asked cheerily.

Alice smiled and nodded, putting the frightened eyes of the apprentice boy out of her mind. She picked two jars from her basket: one ointment for the gums and one powder to help with aching of the joints – both for Sal's elderly father. Alice liked Sal and hoped she was right about the hunters – that they had simply extended their search and would return soon with a healthy stock of meat to trade. But she couldn't help agreeing with Owen.

The tension she had noticed in the village over the past few weeks was even more obvious now. The people here were forest people, just like she was. They too would sense the change in the woods –

small things, hard to pin down – as well as the lack of food and the poor hunting. To Alice it seemed as if everyone knew something terrible was looming, but nobody wished to voice their fears. It made her keener than ever to return to the forest and see what news Storm had from the wolf packs.

She added two pounds of flour and a fist of salt to her basket, thanked Sal and began pushing her way out towards her next stop. The villagers barged and jostled her, casting their sidelong looks as she passed.

Once her rounds were complete, Alice wasted no time in leaving Catchwood and the market-day crowds behind. She wove quickly towards the north gate, nodding to the guard as she passed through the wall of thick wooden stakes that surrounded the village. Immediately she felt the deep relief of being back on the wild mountainside. The breeze flowed over her, lifting her hair and catching in the folds of her skirt. The musty, human smells of the village were swept away, replaced by the sweetness of the pines and the crystalline mountain air.

Alice turned uphill towards the trees and reached out with her Whisperer sense. The tree line altered minutely as a familiar grey silhouette padded into view. Alice smiled. She ran the rest of the way, swinging the basket of supplies at her side, and plunged into the forest, letting its coolness envelop her. Dogwood and sagebrush whipped harmlessly at her legs as she ran. She ducked the low sweeping branches of oaks, and dodged between the slender aspens and pines.

And then Storm was there, grey and black and golden-eyed, nuzzling into her. Alice ran her hands through the thick, soft fur behind her companion's velvety ears. The bond between them pulsed with the warmth of their friendship – and with anticipation: Storm had something to tell her.

You've heard from the wolf packs? Alice said, her words entering Storm's mind directly. She stepped back, sensing that bad news was coming.

There's a trail, said Storm. *Lifeless forest on the*

high ridge – scorched earth and dead trees. It leads to the mountain pass, to the Darklands.

Alice stared blankly off into the pines. Her heart thumped in her chest.

Narlaw, she whispered.

Yes. Storm bowed her head. *We must tell Moraine. And the elders. The village is in danger.*

Alice nodded in a state of shock. Generations had passed since the Narlaw had been banished to the Darklands. They were shape-shifters, beings who lived only to destroy the natural world. Their touch had the power to wither anything that lived. It seemed so wrong to think of such things, especially here in the great forest, with the trees swaying gently and the birds trilling their midday songs overhead.

But the wolves did not lie. And they had smelled the scent of demons.

Together, Alice and Storm moved swiftly through the forest. They had no need for roads or paths. This was their home and it always had been. Even before they had met, before they had been joined by the ancient Whisperer bond, they had each spent their lives in the cool, sweet-smelling shadows of the pine trees. Alice had been chosen as a baby, when the sacred raven had dropped a white feather on the doorstep of her birth home. For Storm it had been different; animals are closer to the earth than humans and are born with the knowledge inside them. But both Alice and Storm had left their families and come to Catchwood to be trained by Moraine.

Alice often wondered about her mother and father, and she knew that Storm also thought about her own parents, sisters and brothers out there in the roaming wolf packs of the forest. Alice felt sad sometimes, not knowing about her family, but this was part of the Whisperer life, and it made her bond with Storm all the more precious. As she walked, she ran her hand over Storm's thick-furred back – a back that rose almost to her chest. It was no wonder the villagers viewed her with fear and suspicion, this young girl from the forest who walked with the wolves.

They continued through the dappled light,

between hanging clusters of pine needles and the ridged bark of the trunks. The forest could give you everything you needed to live: food, shelter, water, even clothing – just as long as you took no more than you required. Greed upset the balance of the wild. As a Whisperer, this was the very first thing that Alice had been taught. And it was the reason why the recent changes in the forest – the lack of prey and plants – had to be taken very seriously.

As they approached the small hollow where their cottage lay, Moraine's voice became audible. She was speaking with a man, but Alice was not close enough to recognize his voice.

Elder Garth, Storm told her. *Perhaps they have heard of the Narlaw already.*

Perhaps, said Alice, through the bond.

William Garth was the village's chief elder. He was a shrewd man and he ran the village well, but Alice couldn't help thinking he had much too high an opinion of himself. As they entered the clearing they found Garth's horse tethered to a tree beyond the small cottage and outhouses. It shied nervously from Storm, and Alice reached out to the beast with her Whisperer sense, attempting to calm him as they passed. She could hear the deep tones of the village elder clearly now, along with Moraine's soft, thoughtful voice. She unlatched the front door and she and Storm entered the cottage, their home.

"If it's a seasonal thing then we must know when it ends…" Garth stopped mid-sentence as Alice and Storm appeared in the doorway. He was seated beside the empty fireplace and his jaw hung open for a second before he composed himself and nodded a silent greeting.

"I see you've finished at the market," said Moraine. "Elder Garth and I were discussing the worrying changes taking place in the forest." She stood in the kitchen area that was part of the large, open living space of the cottage. Behind her, on her favourite perch, sat Hazel, Moraine's tawny owl companion.

Alice shut the door behind her and nodded politely at the elder before addressing Moraine.

"The wolf packs have found something," she said, glancing nervously at Storm. "Signs of Narlaw moving down from the mountain pass."

Moraine narrowed her eyes. "What signs?"

"Dead trees, lifeless earth. The pine sickness seems to originate there, too."

Moraine stared down at the stone-tiled floor in contemplation. She calmly smoothed the folds of her skirt, as she often did when thinking.

"The wolves are sure," said Alice. "The trail leads to the Darklands."

Garth let out a short, incredulous laugh. "Come now. You're letting your imagination get the better of you. There have been no Narlaw here for a hundred years – not in all of Meridina! They were banished forever, despite what your … animal friend claims."

Storm glared at the elder, snorting impatiently, and Garth's smile slipped. He looked to Moraine for reassurance. "Am I right? There can be no serious suggestion of Narlaw here – not in this day and age."

"You must let me think," Moraine said, distractedly. "If the signs are as Alice says, then…"

Garth stood up. "I didn't come here to listen to rumours, I came here for help in returning the forest to its profitable best. Our hunters find nothing to trade and the village is suffering. That is the only problem here. Every school child learns how the Narlaw were defeated by Queen Amina. They cannot return. You of all people should know that."

Alice felt a rush of anger as the elder straightened his coat and strode towards the door. "You can't just ignore the signs," she cried. "The wolves know far more than we do of the forest. If they say the Narlaw are coming, then we have to do something! The hunters may be in danger. We all may be in danger!"

Garth ignored her, turning instead to Moraine as he left. "You ought to keep her under control," he said. "She's a wild one. And when you've figured out what's really wrong with the forest, let me know."

As the door thumped shut behind him, Moraine remained deep in thought.

Alice rushed over, frustration flooding through her like a fever. She couldn't stand the way Garth had spoken to her – as if everything she knew meant nothing simply because she was younger than him. "We have to find the hunters," she said to Moraine. "Something bad has happened, I know it. Storm knows it. We have to do something."

"Wait, child, wait." Moraine raised her hand as if to ward off Alice's words. "We have to think. Perhaps what the wolves saw was caused by something else; a natural sickness we can cure."

"But we can't wait," said Alice. "The hunters are out there. It may be too late already."

Moraine straightened. "You are a novice, Alice, and you will do as I say. Unpack those provisions while I see to my books. There is always something in them that will help." She strode away into the back room that was both her bedroom and study. Her long, greying hair swayed as Hazel swooped silently after her.

Alice remained in the kitchen. She dropped the basket on to the floor as Storm came over to her.

All we need is some evidence that the Narlaw are here, Alice whispered. *Then Moraine will have to believe us and the villagers will send a search party out for the hunters.*

The thought of disobeying Moraine made her stomach churn with nerves, but it had to be done. No one else was going to help the hunters.

And if the Narlaw are coming...? Storm began.

But she didn't need to finish. If the Narlaw were coming, if they were free from the Darklands, then the village, the forest and the whole of Meridina were in danger.

CHAPTER 2

Alice crouched amidst the towering pines, examining the trail left by the missing hunters. She and Storm were halfway up the mountainside already, more than an hour into their search. With Moraine so absorbed in her books, their exit from the cottage had been easy. Alice had simply changed into her forest clothes – loose trousers and a long, deep green coat – and slipped away silently into the trees. She was sure this was the right thing to do, but her conscience bothered her even so; she had never disobeyed Moraine before in such a way.

They had stopped just short of a fork in the track. There was a small clearing ahead, in which lay a fallen juniper tree and the broken stone circle of an old fire pit. Afternoon sunlight slanted through the trees and covered everything in streaks of gold and shadow.

The carpet of pine needles was scuffed haphazardly by boot prints, a sign that the hunters had paused here. Alice could imagine them resting their legs and taking some water before resuming their hunt for deer or rabbit or boar. She rose and circled the clearing, feeling Storm nearby but unable to hear her. She never could. Storm moved like a ghost through the forest, born to the ways of stealth and silence. Like all wolves, she only let you see or hear her when she was ready.

Alice quickly found the hunters' onward trail.

"North," she said quietly, examining the tracks – deeper into the forest, out towards the snowy peaks. The hunters had made no attempt to conceal their passing. And why should they? They had not heard the rumours of Narlaw.

It was a cold, frightening thought. They were hunting for signs of Narlaw, she and Storm – demons from another land, another time.

She felt Storm approaching, then her companion

emerged from the trees, grey-black fur like a thundercloud.

More pine sickness up ahead, said Storm. Her golden eyes narrowed. *We must move quickly and find the hunters before dark if we can.*

She started out immediately, brushing affectionately against Alice as she passed. Alice dug her hand into the thick mane of fur behind Storm's ears and trailed her fingers along her companion's glossy back. It was a good feeling, knowing that Storm was with her, that she was not alone.

The trail climbed gradually through the endless marches of pine, spruce and aspen, and the sky grew dim with the approach of evening. The forest showed new signs of sickness: clusters of disease-blotched trees and then a small brook that had dried up, becoming a stagnant nest for flies. Soon, birdsong was all but gone from the air.

Alice heard a distant howl and Storm paused to return the call. There were wolves throughout the great forest, lone hunters and packs. Storm was set apart from her kind but, unlike Alice among the villagers, she had retained their respect.

It was almost twilight when they emerged from the trees and followed the path up a steep embankment into a broad vale of unhealthy, yellowing grass. Two hundred paces away the tree line resumed, rising sharply towards a pass between two jagged mountain peaks. These northern passes marked the very edge of Meridina, the cold, craggy border between the living world and the Darklands.

From the vale a vast stretch of the Northern Range was visible. Alice looked west, picking out the ruins of forts and castles in the foothills. Now abandoned, they had been built during Queen Amina's reign, when war had raged against the seemingly unstoppable Narlaw. But the queen had banished them, bringing peace to Meridina for more than a hundred years.

And if the Narlaw had returned?

What then?

Alice breathed the cool mountain air into her lungs. Responsibility would fall on her shoulders. She would be called upon to fight, along with all the other Whisperers of Meridina. During the Narlaw Wars, Queen Amina had built an army of Whisperers, hundreds of them banded together against the Narlaw. But how many were there now? Alice had only ever met one other, and that was Moraine. The rest were scattered, unknown to each other; many would be young and inexperienced like her. Alice's training was only half complete. She knew that she could recognize a Narlaw if she came across one – all Whisperers were born with this talent; but to perform the act of banishment was far beyond her. Moraine said she was too impulsive, that she didn't take the meditative ways of the Whisperers seriously, too eager to excel in combat and stealth and to become a wolf of the forest like her companion.

Alice was proud of her eagerness to act. The trouble was, she knew almost nothing of the Narlaw – no one did, it had been so long ago. So what if this was a huge mistake? She was twelve years old, a novice. How could she possibly face the demons from over the mountain?

Some fifty paces away she spotted Storm, tall and rigid, beckoning her. Alice forced all of these doubts to the back of her mind, setting out at a flat run. As she neared, Storm turned and sped towards the tree line.

In the pines, said Storm.

When they reached the trees there were signs of struggle everywhere: snapped branches, flattened undergrowth, footprints all over the track. Alice skirted the edge of the scene with her heart pounding. She dropped to her knees and scoured the earth for a clue to what had happened to the hunters.

The tracks don't lead anywhere, she said.

Demons, said Storm. *The Narlaw leave no trace. They are not animals, not living things like wolves or humankind. They breathe no air, leave no tracks, build no homes. They exist only to destroy.*

Alice tried not to let her fear show, though the bond would carry it to Storm regardless.

The scent is strong, said Storm, turning uphill towards the mountain pass. *We will find them.*

Alice ran to Storm's side. *Let's go,* she said.

The forest changed as they climbed towards the shoulder of the mountain. The undergrowth thinned, rocks appeared between the pines and the trees themselves became thinner, slanted and crooked. The sickness had spread to almost every tree here. Alice breathed heavily, barely keeping pace with Storm, who didn't seem tired at all.

Then Storm stopped abruptly beside a jutting outcrop of rock.

Do you feel it? she asked.

Alice reached out with her Whisperer sense. There was a strange presence in the trees. It rushed towards her, taking on a sickening intensity, as if the air itself was tainted by a skin of oil. Alice drew back, alarmed and afraid.

The demons are close, said Storm.

How close? Alice whispered.

They had climbed all this way to find evidence of Narlaw in the forest, and now here they were in the failing light, on the verge of seeing the demons with their own eyes.

Storm did not answer, instead she crept silently past the rocks. Alice followed. The slow creak of the trees was the only sound. Shadows crowded everywhere, twisting as the trees swayed gently.

Then Storm stopped in her tracks, one paw raised above the ground.

We should go, she said.

Alice stopped beside her. Ahead, on a stretch of level forest, were several large boulders. Around the boulders Alice glimpsed five or six figures. There was no fire, no movement and no talk between the figures. A foul smell drifted on the air. Alice recognized the silhouettes of the hunting party. She edged forwards, but was stopped by a sharp pulse of warning through the bond.

No, said Storm. *We have to get back to the village.*

But it's them, Alice whispered. *They need our help.*

But even as she spoke she realized that these were not the hunters, and that she and Storm had gone too far.

The figures moved between the boulders and Alice felt the demon taint return, creeping over her, polluting her senses. She stared, chest frozen with fear, as the hunters turned towards her slowly. Their eyes opened to reveal a sickly grey glow.

Go! Storm snapped. *Warn the elders!*

What about you? Alice hissed.

I'll lead them away, but you must get to the village!

Then Storm stepped forwards and howled, a long, soul-shivering cry that was answered, seconds later, by one and then two and then a whole chorus of howls from near and far. The wolf packs were coming to her aid.

Alice didn't want to run, she wanted to stay and fight, but there were six Narlaw and just two of them.

She pressed a hand to Storm's side, then broke off and sprinted downhill as Storm charged in the opposite direction. Alice felt the distance grow between them, felt the night close in around her. And over everything, spreading like a blot of ink in water, she felt the Narlaw seeking her out, coming for her down the hillside.

CHAPTER 3

The trees loomed like phantoms as Alice ran. Her boots slid on the litter of pine needles, caught on the roots of trees. Her heart hammered and the forest hissed and creaked and howled around her.

Alice stumbled and skidded down the steep path they had climbed just minutes ago. She listened for sounds of pursuit but heard only chaos in amongst the trees as the wolves and the Narlaw tore in all directions through the night.

A howl went up nearby and Alice ducked behind a crooked pine. A low shape flashed through the undergrowth – a wolf. Next came a blur of limbs, moving faster than anything Alice had ever seen. Both creatures were out of sight in an instant.

Alice stood and resumed her charge downhill,

hoping that the wolves could outrun the Narlaw, that Storm was not in trouble.

She tripped and fell, scrambled up and kept running. Dusky light reached through the trees and she stopped, breathing heavily, at the edge of the grassy vale. Scraps of cloud flew across the sky and the yellowed grass of the vale shone like copper in the half light. Straight across was the quickest way. Alice scanned the vale and was about to run when she caught the slightest movement off to her left: a figure, twenty paces away along the tree line, watching the open ground, waiting. Alice crept back into deeper cover. The figure was tall – a man – and stood with the impossible stillness she had witnessed in the Narlaw camp. This was one of them, a creature she had read about and feared all her life – and it was hunting.

Alice moved slowly along the tree line and away from the watcher. She didn't dare remove her gaze from him, placing her boots in the undergrowth with tortuous precision. Then a howl split the sky elsewhere in the woods. The figure shifted. In a movement that was swift and horrifying, the Narlaw sped across the vale and was gone.

It took a huge effort for Alice to calm her breathing. What would a demon like that do to a wolf if it caught one? What would it do to Storm? Or her? All Alice had to go on were the stories passed down through generations and, according to the histories, these demons had been fought and beaten by the armies of Meridina, by the great Whisperer, Queen Amina. But it seemed the true horror of the Narlaw had been lost in the retelling – their silence and their eerie stillness, followed by such frightening bursts of speed.

Alice peered out into the vale, then back into the pitch black of the forest. She had to get home. No matter what Moraine had thought before, she would have to believe Alice now she had seen the Narlaw with her own eyes. If they didn't warn the villagers then everything the wolves had done for her would have been in vain. She had to be there when Storm returned, too. So Alice placed one foot in front of the other, quickening each time, until once again she was running through the ghostly forest towards home.

The mountainside was broad and the wolves had done their job well. Their cries became distant and infrequent. Alice hoped that meant they had succeeded in drawing the Narlaw away, losing the demons in the deep forest. The alternative was not worth considering.

She reached a familiar part of the forest and paused to catch her breath above a shallow gully that she and Storm had crossed a thousand times before. The sound of her breathing merged with the wind in the treetops. Alice watched and listened. She was almost home, but she could not afford to be careless now.

Somewhere a branch fell and cracked. Had it been blown by the wind, or dislodged by something else? A large bird took to the air nearby, given away only by the beating of its wings. Alice listened, reaching out with her Whisperer sense. She felt a presence; not the bird, but a wolf in the gully: a strange wolf – not Storm. She made her breathing quiet and stayed utterly still until she saw the wolf's shadow creeping, wary and exhausted, down the gully. If she stayed where she was it would pass by without seeing her, but part of her wanted to call out, to make the rest of the journey home with at least this unknown wolf for company. But to give herself away would not be wise. She stayed quiet and hidden.

As the wolf passed by in the gully, Alice felt another presence suddenly emerge, sickening and swift. She gasped as a shadow dropped from nowhere and a furious, howling battle commenced. Wolf and Narlaw grappled. The snarling and gnashing of teeth destroyed the silence of the forest. Alice stayed low, ready to run for her life as the two shadows rolled and twisted below her.

Then all was still. The wolf's cries receded in one eerie final echo. The Narlaw stood, one hand on the wolf's limp body. It seemed as if the wolf was breathing, but Alice couldn't be sure.

She had to go. The demon would see her any time now, surely. But what happened next kept

Alice rooted to the spot.

The Narlaw – its human silhouette – slowly dropped on to its hands and knees. Its body thickened; the shadowy head enlarged and stretched and when it moved again the silhouette was pure wolf. Alice didn't dare to even breathe. The shape-shifter raised its head and sniffed the air. A wolf's nose would detect her easily. She got ready to run, backing away from the gully into more open ground. It had to be now. If she was lucky she may just make it home before the wolf-demon caught her.

And if she was unlucky?

It wasn't worth thinking about. She had to get home. That was all.

Alice rose to her feet. She stepped backwards, keeping the Narlaw-wolf in sight.

Then a hand slipped roughly over her mouth and she was dragged backwards. She kicked out uselessly. There was a rhythmic whispering inside her head, strange words chanted silently that made her legs feel suddenly heavy, as if they were attached to the forest floor, as inanimate as tree stumps.

Alice recognized the words of the stealth wish. She glanced up and saw the tufted outline of a tawny owl on a branch above.

Hazel.

"Hush, dear," Moraine whispered. "The forest will hide us." The incantation didn't falter as she spoke.

Alice allowed herself to be carried away, Hazel deftly swooping from branch to branch above them. They retreated from the gully and the Narlaw did not follow. They were invisible, a part of the forest.

Only when they reached the cottage did Alice feel the weight of the stealth wish rise from her body. She had performed that wish on herself before, but had never been the subject of someone else using it on her. Her body didn't feel her own. She stumbled through the door and would have fallen had Moraine not held her.

"Storm," Alice muttered. "She's still out there."

"I know, dear."

Moraine sat her beside the fire, where the embers flickered grey and red. Moraine looked tired, drained by the effort of their escape. It took skill and strength to commune with the forest, to ask its help and become one with the earth.

"It put the wolf to sleep," said Alice. "I saw it change shape…"

Moraine nodded. "The cottage is protected. We must wait until morning and then warn the village elders." She paused, rubbing her eyes. For an instant she looked lost, as if she still couldn't believe what she had seen. "You were right about the Narlaw, and I am sorry that I doubted you. But you shouldn't have gone into the forest like that. Anything might have happened."

"Storm and the wolves," said Alice. "They drew the demons away. We need to help them."

Moraine shook her head. "It's far too dangerous, now. Storm will know what to do."

Alice wanted to get up, to run back into the forest and not stop until she had her companion beside her again. She couldn't stand being separated from Storm, not knowing if she was scared or hurt. But Alice had been lucky to get home and even she knew that to set out again would be madness. So she perched on the chair by the dying fire and reached out through the stone walls of the cottage, out into the thick shadows of the forest, feeling desperately for Storm and hoping that her friend would return to her soon.

CHAPTER 4

The morning bell tolled slowly in the central courtyard of the Palace of the Sun, signalling the end of the night watch and the changing of the palace guard. Soon the city of Meridar would wake and the palace would be full of noise and colour, its residents rising to their daily duties.

Dawn, however, had already been awake for two hours.

Her head ached from reading by candlelight, poring through the ancient books that Esther had left her: books about healing, folklore and the secrets of the Whisperer sisterhood, scrolls of ancient historical events and the war diaries of Queen Amina.

These war diaries in particular made for

disturbing reading. No one knew where the Narlaw had come from, only that they were not of this world. They had crept into Meridina's borderlands some hundred years ago, targeting each isolated town and village, sinking the entire population of these towns into the ghost-sleep so that no one could flee or warn their neighbours of the invasion. And the Narlaw themselves: lightning fast and as strong as three people. They had overwhelmed Meridina with their vast numbers and fought their way to the palace gates.

A long time had passed since the Narlaw Wars. Queen Amina had banished the demons to the Darklands, but it remained a vital duty of all Whisperers to protect the realm from these Narlaw that had arrived in Meridina like a curse from some other world.

Dawn extinguished the candles on her desk and rubbed her tired eyes. There was so much to learn. If only Esther were still with her to guide her, to help her decipher the arcane language and separate fact from mythology. But Esther had died last winter from the long illness that had plagued her old age, and now Dawn was the Palace Whisperer, the youngest Meridina had ever known. It still felt like madness, looking around at these lavish rooms. She was the foremost Whisperer in Meridina and advisor to King Eneron, a king who was old and frail and unwilling to face up to his royal duties.

Dawn crossed the room to the balcony, where rosy morning light made the city and the palace grounds glow. Here, looking out from the ornate Spiral Tower, she felt as free as she ever did these days. Only here did the weight of her responsibilities begin to lighten. She pretended she was far from the palace, back home in the Southlands, before her Whisperer bond had been confirmed, before they had come and removed her from her beloved, sand-coloured hills and brought her here to be submerged in palace life.

A dark shape flashed in the air nearby and a loud, throaty caw echoed over the courtyards and ornamental gardens.

Where have you been? Dawn whispered, smiling.

Are you up early or out late?

A pair of tremendous black wings batted the air at the end of the balcony as Ebony, Dawn's raven companion, lighted on the balustrade.

Never ask a raven where she goes at night, Ebony replied. *You may not like the answer.* She stretched and then tucked her wings away, cocking her head in amusement. *All is quiet in the palace. Nothing urgent to report.*

And Princess Ona?

Ebony hopped along the balustrade, peering into the anteroom at the cluttered desk. *Ona's fine. There's a new addition to that dizzy-headed court of hers. The son of a wealthy merchant. The princess has taken a liking to him, I think, and, as always, she is blissfully unaware of the mess her father is making of her future kingdom.*

Dawn nodded. Princess Ona was the sole heir to the throne of Meridina, but King Eneron refused to involve her in state affairs. In fact, he had expressly banned Dawn or any other court official from entering the princess's chambers. If things continued in this way, Ona would inherit the kingdom without the faintest idea how to rule. And in the meantime, the king piled more and more duties on to Dawn's inexperienced shoulders.

In the courtyard below, the palace servants were beginning to emerge, reminding Dawn that she would shortly be due at the morning council. She hurried back inside.

I wonder what our dear friend the warden has in store for us this morning, Ebony mused as she flew inside and perched between the carved figurines on the marble mantelpiece.

The palace warden, Lady Tremaine, was in charge of the daily running of the palace and had not missed a single opportunity to criticize Dawn. After nine months in her role, Dawn still wasn't able to ignore the warden's withering remarks.

She took the heavy Palace Whisperer's robe from its place in her dressing chamber and slipped it on over her southern-style tunic and trousers. Immediately, Ebony landed on her shoulder, her talons tight but not sharp through the padding of the robe.

As she trod the wide flagstone corridors towards the king's council chamber, Dawn's head was awash with the details of the day ahead. Only Ebony's calming presence kept her panic at bay.

The council chamber was ominously silent. Alone at the vast rectangular table sat James Valderin, the Head of the Palace Guard. He looked up, nodding politely at Dawn as she entered. Dawn took a seat close to Valderin, feeling Ebony shift impatiently on her shoulder.

The silence stretched and Dawn was on the verge of forcing out some pointless small talk when the double doors at the far end of the room burst open and the palace warden strode in, closely followed by King Eneron himself. Dawn rose to her feet, as did Valderin. They all waited as the king ambled to the head of the table and slumped into his gilded chair.

The warden glanced briefly at the king to see if, for once, he might open the proceedings according to the royal custom; but King Eneron simply stared, glassy-eyed, through the tall chamber windows, out towards the rippling flags on the battlements beyond.

"Well, then," said the warden. "Let us begin." She gracefully seated herself at the right hand of the king and opened a worn leather case that was stacked neatly with papers.

As this was happening, Ebony switched on to Dawn's other shoulder in a brief flurry of flapping.

Lady Tremaine immediately looked up from her papers.

"This is a chamber of council, not a falconry exhibition," she snapped, staring across the table at Dawn. "It would be polite if you could keep your animal under control in the presence of the king."

The presence of the king? whispered Ebony. *The king is barely present himself.*

Dawn might have smiled if she hadn't been pinioned by Lady Tremaine's ferocious glare. She nodded meekly to the warden then turned to address King Eneron. "My apologies, Your Grace. My companion is merely restless after a night spent patrolling the palace grounds at Captain Valderin's request."

The king showed no sign of being offended by Ebony's presence, nor of having heard any word that Dawn had spoken. Unsurprisingly, it was the warden who supplied an answer.

"Patrolling?" she sneered. "Not very thoroughly, it seems. Valderin, tell our resident Whisperer what happened last night."

Now it was Valderin's turn to squirm in his seat.

"Well," he began, turning awkwardly between Dawn and Lady Tremaine, "the palace aqueduct seems to have been damaged. The supply of fresh water from the hill springs is compromised."

"Sabotage," said Lady Tremaine, banging her fist on the table and temporarily startling the king from his reverie. "The palace water supply has been deliberately tampered with."

Through the bond, Dawn felt Ebony mirror her own embarrassment. Security was Valderin's responsibility, but Dawn and Ebony had offered their help and now this didn't look good for any of them.

"So," the warden continued, "how, I'd like to know, did both Head of Guards and our Whisperer's famed companion fail to prevent such a dangerous act of sabotage? Is the king's water supply not worthy of protection?"

Valderin shifted in his chair. "I'll begin an investigation right away," he said.

"See that you do," the warden barked, before turning her attention back to Dawn. "And I would think our Palace Whisperer had enough to do without playing at guard duty as if it were a game. You should stick to healing and scholarly pursuits from now on. It's a shame Esther didn't teach you that much before she passed away."

Dawn felt her cheeks burn. She had been trying to help and, again, she received nothing but condescension. She wanted to stand and yell at the warden, to tell her that she hadn't asked for this job and nor did she want it. She wished Esther were still alive, so she didn't have to put up with this pressure and cruelty every day – especially from someone who was supposed to be helping her.

From then on Dawn remained quiet, brushing off all of the barbed comments Lady Tremaine had to offer. She listened closely as Valderin laid out the details of the sabotaged aqueduct. It was a strange occurrence indeed, and no one around the council table could guess who might have wanted the palace water supply stopped.

Dawn scribbled notes, and anger and determination surged through her bond with Ebony.

She would go with Valderin after the meeting and take a look for herself – no matter what Lady Tremaine said. She was a Whisperer. Protecting the kingdom was her job, not just poring over old books and keeping records.

When the council ended, she bowed to the king and left the chamber feeling as deflated and over-worked as usual.

That went well, said Ebony, stretching her wings.

Dawn allowed herself the faintest of smiles, wondering for the thousandth time how on earth her life had grown so complicated.

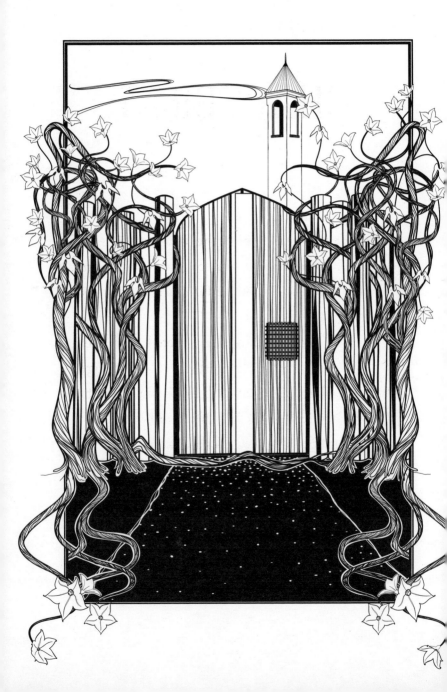

CHAPTER 5

Alice opened her eyes to the first dim light of morning. The cottage was colourless and grey. Shadows stretched from the furniture and the roof beams.

"You're awake," Moraine greeted her from the kitchen. "Good. We must go to the village." She carefully placed a small glass vial into her embroidered leather satchel, then another.

Alice rubbed her tired eyes and sat up. Her back ached from her awkward position in the armchair and the guilt of having slept the night away came upon her suddenly. She had slept, warm and safe in the cottage, whilst Storm had been out in the forest running from the Narlaw. Alice reached out for Storm's presence, but there was nothing. She glanced urgently around, and then looked imploringly at Moraine, who simply shook her head.

"Not yet, my dear," Moraine said. "Come. We have to warn the elders."

Hazel swooped through the canopy above them, keeping watch, and Moraine's eyes darted up to her companion as the pair silently communicated. If she was angry with Alice, she did not show it. Alice peered out into the trees. The chill light of dawn made the forest seem empty and deserted. But it was not empty. There were creatures out there, demons whose sole desire was to lay waste to the mountainside.

There were no wolf cries on the morning air, nothing but silence when Alice reached out with her Whisperer sense. To keep panic from rising up inside, she concentrated on the task at hand: to protect the village and somehow banish the Narlaw back to the Darklands. No such thing had been attempted for a hundred years. Moraine knew the theory, but she had never tested herself against a real Narlaw. She had never had the chance. Once, Moraine had hinted at the existence of an elderly Whisperer, a survivor from Queen Amina's time hiding somewhere in the northern mountains. Perhaps she could help? But this was little more than a rumour. To perform the act of banishment seemed impossible now.

Alice realized with a jolt that this was what being a Whisperer meant. This was what she had been born for, but it filled her with a deep and terrible apprehension. She followed Moraine out of the trees towards the village. At the gate the guard straightened, surprised at their sudden appearance.

"We're here to see the elders," Moraine told him. "Please tell them to ring the bell for council."

The guard stood dumbstruck as the two Whisperers strode past him, Hazel gliding low above their heads. Alice hurried along beside Moraine, between the tightly packed cottages and barns, the shuttered stables and the occasional smoking chimney. They crossed the market square, under the festival tree to the squat grey bell tower of the village hall.

As they reached the heavy, wooden door of the hall, the guard caught up with them. He was out of breath. "Elder Garth is not yet awake," he said. "If you could just wait in the inn, then perhaps…"

Moraine rounded on him. "We are here to protect the village," she said, "from the demons now at large in these mountains. I suggest you unlock this door. I shall ring the bell for council myself."

The guard stuttered wordlessly. He was a young man and Alice felt sorry for him. Under Moraine's powerful gaze he eventually fumbled a key from his tunic and climbed the steps to unlock the door. Inside, Moraine stalked straight past the rows of benches to the base of the bell tower and began climbing the tight spiral staircase. All of her bookish uncertainty was gone now that she had seen the Narlaw with her own eyes.

Alice made her way to the raised platform at the front. Her footsteps echoed on the polished wooden floor. Seconds later the bell tolled urgently overhead. Three rings, then a pause, then three more, the pattern repeated over and over.

It didn't take long before a small crowd of villagers had formed outside. The air hummed with the after-song of the bell as Moraine joined Alice at the door. Below them, the crowd split to allow Elder William Garth to the front.

"What on earth is going on here?" He glared at them irritably. "Please tell me you have not woken the village to spread more ridiculous rumours."

Alice stepped forwards angrily, but Moraine shot her a fearsome glance and she held her tongue.

"I've called a council," Moraine said. "Last night Narlaw were encountered in the forest. They have taken the forms of the missing hunters."

Several of the gathered villagers gasped. A shout went up asking whether the hunters still lived.

"They are in the ghost-sleep," Moraine replied. "Alive but at the mercy of the Narlaw. The Narlaw who have stolen the hunters' likenesses must be banished from Meridina before the sleep can be lifted."

More anxious cries issued from the crowd, but above them came Elder Garth's humourless laughter. "Not this again," he said. "It is nothing but hearsay, which I refuse to respond to. Especially when it is spread by … wild animals."

"Those wild animals saved me!" Alice cried out without thinking. "They're the only reason we were able to warn you at all – you should be thankful!"

Garth stared at her, red-faced in shock. He turned to Moraine. "How dare this child speak to me in such a way? And how dare you enter the village hall without permission? Everyone go home. Go about your business, there is no emergency…"

But by now there were loud exchanges passing through the crowd. There was talk of a rescue party for the hunters; some claimed this was a Whisperer ruse; some even called for the complete abandonment of the village.

"Quiet!" Moraine bellowed over the throng. "Quiet, please! Alice is right. The wolves have given us some time. Not much, so we must prepare immediately for a Narlaw attack and send word to the palace at Meridar."

The crowd swelled and grew increasingly restless. Two more elders pushed their way to the front and joined in secretive conversation with Garth.

Alice placed a hand on Moraine's arm. "What should we do?" she asked. "No one is listening."

"We must do our duty, dear, and protect the village."

"And the banishment?" Alice asked.

Moraine smiled, but her eyes betrayed her doubt. "We will practise," she said. "We will send to the palace for help and we will seek out a friend of mine – a very old friend who lives here in the mountains."

"The mountains?" asked Alice. "Does your friend know banishment?"

Before Alice could press Moraine further, a scream rose above the noise of the crowd, followed by a chorus of panicked, urgent cries. From the steps of the hall she could just make out the disturbance: people waving wildly, brandishing sticks of firewood or whatever they could lay their hands on.

Was it the Narlaw? Had they come already?

A howl split the air, a sound that Alice felt rather than heard. She leaped from the steps and barged through the crowd, elbowing her way until she was out in the open, staring past a line of armed villagers at the three wolves who had arrived in the market square. The grey-black fur of the lead wolf made her heart skip.

"Stop!" she shouted. "Stop! They're friends!"

She charged past the villagers and threw her arms around Storm. Relief flooded between them.

I thought they'd taken you, she whispered. *I thought they'd put you to sleep.*

Not me, said Storm. *Two others, but not me.*

I'm so glad you're safe, said Alice.

Storm licked her cheek. *And I'm glad you made it back*, she said. *You must be part wolf after all.*

Alice smiled. *Part wolf or part crazy*, she said. *I saw a Narlaw. It changed shape and put a wolf to sleep. How are we going to fight them, Storm?*

I don't know, Storm replied. *We counted six demons in the forest, but more may come. Soon they will regroup and attack the village.*

Come on, said Alice. She led Storm and the other two wolves towards the hall. The crowd parted with a murmur of awe. At the steps they found Moraine deep in conversation with the elders. Garth was nodding thoughtfully. He looked embarrassed, like a small child who has realized his own foolishness.

"Storm," Moraine said, smiling. "Come inside, both of you. We have much to do."

Moraine drew up a letter explaining all that had happened and requesting urgent assistance. She addressed it to the Palace Whisperer in Meridar. Moraine's signature was joined by that of Elder Garth. Alice was also asked to sign.

"It was you and Storm who alerted us to the threat," Moraine said. "You should sign too."

Alice wrote her name as tidily as she could with the stiff quill pen. She had never signed anything before and felt foolish doing so. But Moraine watched her with approval.

Storm had spoken with the two wild wolves,

who now paced impatiently around the edges of the hall. The letter was sealed and fastened inside a leather tube. Storm carried it in her jaws to the taller and leaner wolf, and the two wild wolves left the hall immediately.

They are the fastest on the mountain, Storm said. *The palace will hear from us by nightfall.*

Alice relayed this to Moraine and the elders.

"Good," Moraine said. "Now we must prepare the ward."

Alice stood close to Storm, absently running her hand along her companion's sleek back. They were outside the village, beside the high protective wall. Moraine crouched on the grass, examining the contents of her satchel as Hazel circled high overhead.

They had left the elders to deal with the agitated crowds. Every now and then a small party of villagers set out from the nearby north gate. Word was being sent to the isolated farms and the mountainfolk were being called in to the relative safety of the village walls.

"Here," Moraine said.

Alice took a vial of clear liquid. She had done this before. A protective ward was one of the most vital Whisperer skills. Like all such rituals it involved an exchange, a gift offered to the earth and, if done correctly, a favour obtained in return. In this case the favour was protection.

Moraine nodded solemnly to Alice, who returned the nod. They then set off slowly in opposite directions around the wall.

Alice silently chanted the arcane words and let a drop of the liquid fall to the ground at each step. Behind her, all along the wall, green shoots began to crack the surface of the soil. She continued, deep in concentration, speaking directly to the earth, reaching out with her senses to the living world in a way that only a Whisperer could.

The shoots grew and twisted, waist high, then to shoulder height, clinging to the wooden stakes of the wall. Alice crossed paths with Moraine, but they did not speak or even look up at one another. The stalks reached the top of the wall and small, white, star-shaped flowers began to blossom.

Alice let the liquid fall. She paced and chanted. When she met Moraine the second time the two of them stopped, silently entreating the earth in perfect unison. The old language left their tongues, the ritual came to an end and Moraine raised her head.

"Can you feel it?" she asked.

Alice nodded. The ward was there, a new presence in her mind as if another person – a Whisperer or companion perhaps – had arrived nearby. It was a shimmering circle, full and strong, and if it were broken both she and Moraine would feel it instantly.

"It's broader than a ward should be," Moraine said. "Fragile. But if the Narlaw break it then at least we will have some warning."

They left the village and headed into the woods towards the cottage. Alice glanced back at the newly flowered wall. The village had never looked so beautiful; or, indeed, so vulnerable.

In the cottage kitchen, Alice waited for Moraine. The forest creaked and whispered outside, shaken by the powerful breath of the wind. Storm was out there, keeping watch with Hazel. Alice imagined the Narlaw darting through the trees, turning streams into mud and dust at their touch. She felt the isolation of her mountain home more than ever. There would be no help from the palace for at least two days; until then, the fate of the village depended on them, and them alone.

Moraine emerged from her study. "Come," she said.

Alice noticed the difference in the way Moraine held herself, a forced briskness that spoke of uncertainty, or even fear. Together they stepped out into the yard. The wind had grown strong, whipping every which way and bending the treetops as if they were blades of grass. Alice looked to Storm, who patrolled slowly at the edge of the clearing.

Do not fear, said Storm. *You are safe. Free to learn.*

Thank you, she whispered back.

Moraine led her a short way into the woods, to where two wooden benches lay opposite each other and woven charms hung from the trees.

"You have come close," Moraine said, taking one of the benches. "But you've never fully merged with the earth, not in the way necessary for the act of banishment."

"No," said Alice. This had always been the hardest aspect of her training, the one requiring most patience and subtlety. Alice took the other bench, wishing that the Narlaw could be fought and banished using physical skills, or her knowledge of the forest alone.

"Like a ward or a stealth wish," Moraine said, "you must reach out to the earth – the earth from which all life came. But now you must reach out with your whole self, and become a channel for the earth's great power."

Alice nodded solemnly. She knew what was demanded of her and had attempted it many times, always falling short, always lacking the stillness or the concentration required. She was too easily distracted, too alert to the physical forest around her, to Storm's constant presence. And she had grown used to Moraine's patient, gentle ways, but she could no longer afford to fail at this. Moraine could not tackle the Narlaw by herself.

Alice closed her eyes. The forest shook around her like an angry tide. She tried to empty her head of thoughts, to let the cool wind engulf her, to let the soil merge with her feet. She ignored Storm's gently shifting presence back in the clearing. *Give in*, she urged herself, *give your whole self to the earth*. Storm receded slowly. All she could hear was the roar of the wind. Then the earth beneath her began to shine with life. Alice drew closer to its presence, letting any thought that came into her head be dragged away by the wind. The earth's presence grew stronger. She opened herself to it, the life-giver and the root of all things. And now the wind was gone and there was only silence and warmth. She was close. She felt nothing but an immense stillness. It was frightening and beautiful – to be lost and to be part of the great earth all at once. For an instant she felt pride, like a pinprick through this earth trance, and that feeling alone made her concentration waver. Then a voice broke in and the earth's deep presence rushed away. Alice opened her eyes to the jarring, swaying forest. Moraine was standing over her, Hazel like a sentinel on her outstretched arm.

And there was Storm.

Narlaw, she said. *They have attacked a party of villagers at the forest edge.*

Alice stood, unsteady on her feet.

"You were close, child." Moraine laid a hand on her shoulder. "I could feel it."

Alice tried to smile, but she was filled with fear.

"I wished to send Hazel to my friend Soraya for help," said Moraine. "But there's no time." She took Alice firmly by the shoulders. "We will go to the villagers' aid," she said. "But if anything should happen… If I… Well, then you must seek help from Soraya at Blind Crag. Do you understand?"

Alice nodded, shocked at the suggestion that something might happen to Moraine. "If it comes to that, I'll find her," she said. "I'll bring help, I promise."

Moraine nodded. "Good. Now…"

She turned.

Hazel had already taken flight, leading the way towards the stricken villagers. On the harsh wind, Alice heard a distant cry of alarm.

Are you ready? Storm asked, her golden eyes glowing.

I'm ready, said Alice, though she did not feel it.

Storm snorted and nuzzled into her. Then they ran together, into the woods.

CHAPTER 6

The forest flashed by, blurred and murky as if it were a dream. Alice fought hard to stay steady on her feet. Her attempt at the earth trance had left her drained and disoriented.

Moraine slowed to let her catch up. "When we arrive, you must stay clear of the demons," she told Alice. "Help the villagers to safety. That's all."

"But how will you fight them alone?" Alice asked.

Moraine stared straight ahead as she ran. "I have prepared for this all my life. Now comes the test."

Alice felt her heart lurch in fear. Storm and Hazel were nowhere to be seen and the shouts of the villagers were much louder now, coming from a steep section of forest up ahead, near the ruins of an old cottage. Everything was moving too fast.

"There!" Moraine called out.

Shadows flitted between the trees and Alice found a new burst of speed, a reserve of energy. The crumbling grey stone of the cottage came into view and she felt Storm close by. Then she was there, face to face with the Narlaw.

The demon wore a familiar form, a tall woman with curly blonde hair – one of the missing hunters. But the sockets of its eyes glowed with unearthly grey light and the sickening wrongness of its presence invaded all of Alice's senses.

There were four villagers there, one of whom lay unconscious at the Narlaw's feet. The demon gripped the man's wrist with a powerful hand and a boy, Owen from the marketplace, had the comatose man by the legs. A terrible tug-of-war was taking place.

"Get the villagers away!" Moraine ordered as she arrived. "Get them to safety no matter what." Even as she ran into the fray, Moraine had closed her eyes, beginning her approach to the earth trance.

Storm went straight for the Narlaw, snarling and

darting in to try and break its grip on the man while avoiding the demon's touch. Hazel attacked with wings spread and talons bared. The Narlaw swept its free arm through the air with awesome power and speed, driving both companions back at every attempt.

Alice ran to where the other two villagers stood, transfixed by the fight. She grabbed the first, an elderly man, by the arm. "You have to go!" she shouted.

The man ignored her, simply staring aghast at the scene before him.

Alice tried the woman standing beside him. "Get him out of here," she said. "Get back to the village."

"But my husband..." the woman said, staring hopelessly at the man at the Narlaw's feet.

"We'll help him," Alice promised. "But you have to go."

Owen cried out as the Narlaw swung a fist at him and Alice charged in to help free the stricken man. She grabbed the man's right leg and hauled with all her strength. Owen glanced across at her, wide-eyed.

"You knew?" he shouted. "You knew the demons had come?"

"I tried to warn the elders," Alice panted, struggling to maintain her grip. "They wouldn't listen."

Owen turned away from her, shaking his head and gritting his teeth. The Narlaw's strength was unnatural. It took everything they had just to stop it from dragging the man away.

Alice glanced at Storm, who shot her a decisive look.

Get ready, Storm said.

Alice tightened her grip and nodded to Owen, who seemed to understand.

Storm pounced with her jaws wide and sank them deep into the Narlaw's wrist. The demon's grip loosened and the man slid from its grasp, toppling Alice and Owen in the process.

"Storm!" Alice shouted.

Storm stumbled away, retching violently and

shaking her head at the taste of Narlaw flesh.

The demon turned on Storm, but Hazel renewed her swooping attacks, going for the demon's neck, trying to keep it away from Storm and the others. By now Moraine was deep in the earth trance, kneeling on the forest floor, oblivious to what was happening around her. She would be reaching out, trying to hold the Narlaw's presence close as the earth channelled through her.

"Help me!"

Alice turned. It was Owen, trying to drag the comatose man away into the trees on his own. The other two villagers had finally fled. Alice stood, torn three ways. Storm was hurt, the villagers needed her to help them back to safety and Moraine was completely exposed. She called to Storm: *Run! Come back with me!*

Storm looked up; her eyes were pale, confused by the venomous touch of the demon. But she blinked and focused and saw the Narlaw advancing, still harried by Hazel. She darted, stumbling like a cub, across the clearing to Alice's side.

Alice joined Owen and together they lifted the man so they could carry him across both their shoulders. Storm was too disoriented to help.

It's all right, Alice whispered, straining under the weight of the man. *We'll get back to the village. Moraine will be fine.*

But as she glanced back she realized with a terrible jolt that this was not the case. The Narlaw swung its powerful fist and struck Hazel out of the air, sending her thumping into the stone wall of the abandoned cottage. Hazel fell to the ground with a screech.

"No!" Alice cried as the demon advanced on Moraine.

She dropped the unconscious man and sprinted back.

"Stop!" cried Owen.

But Alice raced on.

Moraine jerked suddenly, shaking her head. Her link with the earth had failed. She saw the Narlaw only paces away and tried to rise from her knees, but it was too late.

The demon placed a hand on her forehead and Moraine crumpled instantly to the ground. Into the ghost-sleep.

Alice cried out breathlessly as she ran and Hazel shrieked in torment at the sudden loss of her bond with Moraine.

The Narlaw lifted Moraine as if she were nothing more than a baby. Then it turned and bounded away, vanishing into the shaking pines.

CHAPTER 7

Only once before had Dawn climbed to the summit of the north wall. Years ago, during the early days of her training, Esther had brought her here to witness the fortifications and the palace's complex waterworks. Now, as she toiled up the exposed stone staircase that clung to the interior of the wall, Dawn remembered why she had not returned since.

A dizzying distance below, vast water tanks filled a courtyard that was under constant shadow of the wall and the towering spires of the palace. The engineers and attendants working at ground level appeared like insects from this height. Dawn gripped the rope handhold and tried not to look down, placing her feet carefully on the worn stone steps. Ebony was already at the top, peering out from the battlements. James Valderin was up there too, no stranger to the precarious walkways of the palace's outer defences.

Dawn reached the top and received the full blast of the wind and the glorious view all at once. The craggy hills of the uplands stretched into the distance, where they blurred and met with the forested mountain ranges of the far north. The nearest of the hilltops, crowned with rocks, was the source of the palace water supply. From its natural springs, the main aqueduct carried water directly to the palace.

Someone's feeling giddy, Ebony said, flapping on to Dawn's shoulder.

Well, not all of us can fly, Dawn replied. She hadn't realized how tightly she'd been gripping the stone battlements.

Valderin was halfway along the wall by now, his blue guard-captain's cape flapping manically in the wind. Dawn set off after him; she couldn't let herself be overcome by fear. Each time the wind gusted, however, she found herself clutching at the wall beside her.

Trust your feet, said Ebony. *The parapet is more than wide enough.*

Dawn didn't reply. Valderin had halted up ahead and was leaning through what seemed to be a huge gap in the wall.

"The aqueduct," said Valderin as Dawn approached. "You can see the damage for yourself."

Dawn peered cautiously out and her head instantly began to spin. She focused, ignoring her churning stomach as the wall plunged some hundred feet to the valley floor. The aqueduct lay a short distance below, spanning the valley from the hillside to the palace wall, passing through to feed the water tanks. Except the water was not reaching the wall; instead it cascaded into the valley through a ragged hole in the aqueduct.

There were engineers at work already, laying wooden supports and clambering across the damaged structure with blocks of stone and buckets of wet mortar. Dawn was about to ask how they got there when she noticed the rope ladder dangling just below her feet. A pulley system was being used to lower masonry and timber to the work site.

"Shall we take a closer look?" Valderin asked.

Dawn stared, aghast, at the rope ladder. She didn't have to climb down, surely. She could see well enough from where she was. Then she thought of Lady Tremaine. What if word got back to her that Dawn hadn't dared go down, or something on the aqueduct was overlooked?

"Yes," Dawn found herself saying. "We should inspect the damage."

She took a deep breath and lowered herself on to the first swaying rung of the rope ladder.

Her sense of duty carried her down to the aqueduct, somehow overriding the horror she felt at being suspended over such a terrible drop.

As soon as she reached solid ground, Ebony landed on her shoulder in a gesture of pride and support. On shaky legs, Dawn approached an engineer and requested a report on the damage. The woman led her and Valderin to a discarded pile of wood.

"This was part of the arch support," the engineer

told her. "The rest of it's down on the valley floor."

Dawn picked up a warped length of timber.

"It looks rotten," she said.

The engineer shook her head. "These supports were replaced only six months ago. Look here," she pointed out a strange pattern of erosion at the broken end of the support. "It's almost as if something burned through it."

"And what could have done this?" Valderin asked.

The engineer shrugged. "I don't know, sir."

Dawn examined the burn marks. Something nudged at a memory deep in the back of her mind.

Ebony seemed to sense the direction of her thoughts.

There are creatures who destroy with their very touch, she said.

Dawn nodded. She glanced at Valderin, who gave her a questioning look.

"Thank you," Dawn said to the engineer before striding back towards the rope ladder, followed closely by Valderin.

"What is it?" he asked.

"Nothing clear enough to speak out loud. First we have to find out who was here last night. If anyone suspicious was sighted."

"The guards have already been questioned. Only the usual servants and water-tank attendants were seen in the vicinity. The merchant's son, Yusuf, passed through the courtyard also."

Dawn paused with one foot on the rope ladder.

"Yusuf? What would he be doing in this part of the palace?"

"Lost, perhaps? He's new to the palace, apparently." Valderin narrowed his eyes in thought. "No. You're right. We should question him."

Dawn nodded and began the sickening climb back towards the looming battlements.

Valderin gave orders for his guards to scour the palace for Yusuf. He was the newest member of Princess Ona's inner circle and, if Ebony was right, the object of the princess's affections.

"We will go straight to Ona's quarters," Dawn

said, striding through the busy servants' corridors that linked the north wall to the east wing of the palace. She hoped the urgency of their search would overrule King Eneron's ban on contact with the princess.

Valderin gathered a small group of guards as they went, so that they arrived in the east wing as a formidable group.

The tall doors that led into Ona's quarters were closed and before them stood two of King Eneron's personal bodyguards, the Guards of the Sun. Their red uniforms and blazing gold helmets gave them an imperious look, and the stern expressions they wore suggested a high level of self-regard.

"Open the doors," Valderin ordered. "We are here to conduct a search of the princess's quarters."

The king's guards glared, unmoving. Each one held a tall spear. The weapons were gold-tasselled and highly ornamental, but their blades looked sharp and perfectly deadly.

"I said open these doors," Valderin barked. "I am the Head of Guards and this is a matter of urgency!"

The guard on the left spoke first, a tall man with bulging arms: "We answer only to the king," he said. "No one may pass without our lord's express permission."

Valderin strode forwards as if to force the doors open himself and the two guards flashed into action, crossing their spears in front of him and blocking his way. Valderin stopped short. His own palace guards drew their swords, awaiting the order to attack.

"How dare you take arms against me!" Valderin raged. "There is a saboteur at large. The king himself may be in danger and you presume to bar me from these quarters?"

"Sir," the second guard – a short, agile-looking woman – spoke. "A signed pass from the king will suffice. Until then we are duty bound to seal these doors."

Valderin snorted angrily and his guards bristled behind him. Dawn stood by, infuriated and scared. King Eneron's mad wish to keep his daughter from the world was about to cause bloodshed in his own palace. She could see Valderin growing more and more irate. His authority had been questioned and his pride hurt in full view of his own retainers. She had to do something before things escalated beyond anyone's control.

"Please," she stepped between the two parties and addressed both sides in what she hoped was a calm and confident tone. "Commander Valderin, Guards of the Sun; we are each doing our duty to the king and the safety of the palace is our shared concern. I acknowledge the king's decree protecting the privacy of Princess Ona and will seek his permission to enter in the proper way. Our cause is urgent, however, and I, as Palace Whisperer, would be grateful if you would allow a message to be passed to the princess while I seek the king's permission."

The king's guards glanced at her, barely taking their eyes from Valderin's guards.

"Commander Valderin," said Dawn. "Please stand your people down."

She felt a deep flush of nerves and embarrassment at issuing such an order – and to a man twice her age, a man armed and experienced where she was simply a girl from the Southlands.

But to her surprise Valderin stepped away, and with a nod he drew his guards back. Swords slid back into scabbards. The tall spears of the Sun Guard uncrossed at the door.

"A message is permitted if the emergency is true," the woman guard said.

Dawn nodded in thanks and asked politely for paper and a quill. As Valderin led his guards away to expand the search for Yusuf, she drafted a note to Princess Ona and handed it to the guards at the door.

"Please see that she reads it immediately," Dawn said.

The guard nodded and Dawn strode away with her pulse racing and the sensation of having got away with something that she really shouldn't have. But what chance was there of the princess responding to her letter? Very slim, Dawn thought, if Ona was as spoilt and flighty as her reputation suggested.

Well, said Ebony, as they marched away. *I have to say I'm impressed.*

Flattery doesn't suit you, Dawn whispered, smiling despite herself. *Anyway, we still have the king to deal with. I'd better do this alone. You know how the warden is.*

Ebony hopped from one of Dawn's shoulder to the other. *Sadly, I do,* she muttered. With a caw, she flapped to an open window and sprang into the air, soaring up and up towards the intricate curves of the Spiral Tower.

The king's reluctance to see Dawn was no surprise. But even the warden recognized the importance of finding the merchant's son, and Dawn was soon admitted to Eneron's chambers.

The rooms were opulent and dark. Thick carpets covered every inch of the floor and candles flickered weakly in the recesses around the walls. The king slouched before a crackling fire, barely awake.

"Your Grace." Dawn curtsied. "Thank you for agreeing to see me."

The king did not respond, but continued to

glower silently at the dance of flames in the hearth.

"I have come with a request, Your Grace." Dawn paused, gathering her courage. "I wish to be admitted to Princess Ona's chambers."

The instant she uttered Ona's name a shroud seemed to lift from over the king. He turned, shocked and angry, his hands clawing at the armrests of his chair.

"You request what?" His words rolled across the drawing room like thunder. "That I – the king of Meridina – overturn my royal decree?"

He lurched up from his chair, swaying on his feet as he did so. He was old and unsteady, but he radiated absolute power.

Dawn had never seen him this way before. She stepped back instinctively, opening her mouth, but only a stuttering nothing emerged.

"I will not have my daughter ruined by the machinations of you, you…" King Eneron glared at Dawn as he searched for the words. "You petty, ungrateful people. You spiteful, shallow courtiers."

Dawn lowered her eyes. She was frightened, but

needed to make him understand. Was it treason to argue with a king? She took a deep breath. It had to be said.

"The kingdom is in danger, Your Grace. Princess Ona may be able to help. I would only speak with her briefly, and I promise—"

"Out!" bellowed the king. "Out of my sight."

He stumbled backwards into his chair and sat down heavily, a startled expression breaking through the fury for an instant.

"Your Grace…"

"Out!" he cried.

Dawn curtsied hurriedly and left, with King Eneron's rage echoing behind her. She ignored Lady Tremaine's smug remarks as she rushed, red-faced, through the reception room and away towards the safety and sanity of the Spiral Tower.

When Dawn arrived she was immediately greeted by Ebony, who came swooping across the anteroom.

You have a guest, Ebony whispered.

A figure stood in the far corner, a woman – or rather, a girl – with her back to the door, dressed in a long hooded robe the colour of a twilit sky. Dawn closed the door behind her and only then did the girl turn.

She had blond hair, pulled back into a tight bun, and a face that Dawn recognized immediately, although she had only ever seen it from afar. Dawn stared mutely across the chamber for a moment before recovering herself.

"Princess Ona?" she said.

"I received your message," said the princess, with a tremor of anxiety in her voice. "Is Yusuf well? Is he safe?"

There was such concern and generosity in the princess's gaze that Dawn felt the immediate urge to protect her. But to have made it here alone and unnoticed also showed true resourcefulness and bravery. Perhaps Ona was not the frivolous young girl people thought her to be.

"We're still searching for Yusuf," Dawn said. "That's why I needed to speak to you, to find out when you saw him last."

Princess Ona's eyes widened. "I haven't seen him since yesterday, at noon. We played chess together and then he left to arrange the re-shoeing of his horse at the stables. You don't think he's come to harm, do you? I couldn't stand it if something happened to him while he was a guest of mine."

"I don't know," said Dawn. "I hope not. But what you've told me will help the search a great deal."

Ona smiled warily. She glanced at the door, as if afraid someone might barge in and find her there. Dawn shared the princess's fears, but she couldn't help thinking that it was not Ona, but she who would find herself in trouble should this secret meeting be discovered.

"We'll search the stables right away," said Dawn. "Perhaps now you should return to your quarters?"

"He's such a gentleman," said Princess Ona, bowing her head as she crossed towards the door. "So quiet and clever. We have to find him."

Dawn nodded in sympathy. But if Yusuf had re-shoed his horse it implied he was preparing to leave town – another piece of evidence against him. Perhaps Ona was deluding herself, or perhaps the boy was simply a skilled actor and spy.

The princess raised her hood in readiness to leave and Dawn studied her closely. The princess was no fool – naïve perhaps, but certainly no fool. She was convinced of Yusuf's good nature, so maybe things were more complicated than they seemed.

Help her return to her quarters unseen, Dawn whispered to Ebony. *I'll find Valderin.*

Ona pressed her hand into Dawn's and Dawn did her best to smile reassuringly. Ona's expression was so honest, so unguarded, that Dawn felt strangely moved by her. The princess was scared and trying her best to be brave. In that way she was not so different from Dawn herself.

Once Ebony and Princess Ona were gone, Dawn made her way as fast as she could down the stairs and passageways of the Spiral Tower. She stopped a palace guard on the way and sent word for Valderin to meet her at the stables. A dark feeling crept over her as she descended, one she could not ignore.

The destruction of the aqueduct came back into focus and she thought again of those marks, searing through the strong timber; she remembered Esther's slow, rich voice: *a demon can destroy any living thing it touches.*

In the lower levels of the palace all was in shadow, the towers and ramparts blotting out the sun. The chill Dawn felt as she walked was different. She was full of dread and a strange, unshakeable certainty.

When she arrived she found the stables already busy with palace guards. Valderin had got there first and by the look on his face he had found something.

"Come," he said.

In an unused corner of the sprawling stables, Yusuf was curled like a baby on a bed of straw. He was breathing, but so faintly he seemed barely alive. Valderin's guards looked on. There was an air of confusion and fear. The horses stamped and whinnied in their stalls.

Dawn crouched and laid a hand on Yusuf's forehead. She felt for his presence, his living being, in the way Esther had shown her. The boy was there, inside, but far away and very weak. There was a taint on him that made Dawn flinch away.

This was the confirmation of her fears: Yusuf's form had been stolen by a Narlaw.

For the first time in a century there were demons in Meridina.

CHAPTER 8

Dawn strode across the flagstone floor of the palace infirmary. A nurse walked with her, a scarf covering her nose and mouth. Just one bed was occupied in this ward and it was guarded by one of Valderin's retainers. Another guard stood sentry at the door.

The guard glanced nervously at the nurse as they approached. "Is he contagious?" he asked, gesturing to the scarf masking her face.

The nurse said nothing, simply bending over the unconscious boy and touching his head gently to check his temperature.

"We don't know," said Dawn. "But it's best you leave us for a moment."

The guard nodded, making his way towards his colleague at the exit.

"You see," Dawn said quietly. "He's alive."

Princess Ona slid the scarf from her face and peered down at Yusuf.

"He looks peaceful," she said. "Are you sure he's not in pain?"

"All the old accounts say the same thing: a dreamless sleep. When he wakes he'll feel confused and hungry, but that's all."

"If he wakes," the princess said.

"We must find the Narlaw that did this. Only banishing it will save him."

Ona touched Yusuf's slim dark hand. He was no older than she or Dawn.

"His father is a merchant," Ona said, "on the desert borders. He sent Yusuf here, hundreds of miles north, to further his education, to learn about the world. He was so different from everyone else at court, from the young nobles father forced me to associate with. Not petty or greedy or condescending to the servants."

She looked up at Dawn, her eyes misting with tears. "He was kind. A real friend. He didn't deserve this."

"I know," said Dawn. She too had been sent from her home in the south, thrust into this world of power and politics and courtly behaviour. She felt ashamed for having assumed Yusuf's guilt. He had simply been unlucky, singled out by the Narlaw.

"But we'll find it," Ona said. A sudden fire replaced the sadness in her eyes. "We'll find the demon and bring Yusuf back to life. Swear it with me."

Dawn felt the other girl's passion in her own heart. She was the Palace Whisperer, the defender of the kingdom. She would not – could not – let her people down.

"I swear," she said, holding Ona's gaze.

A black shape intruded on the corner of her vision. Dawn turned. It was Ebony, on the outside ledge of the window.

"We must go," Dawn said, glancing furtively at the door to the ward.

Ona nodded and slipped the scarf back over her face.

Ebony cawed from outside. *The warden,* she said. *On the stairs.* She flew past the windows, making the sunlight flash with her shadow.

"Come on," Dawn whispered urgently, leading Ona back across the ward.

But it was too late to escape unnoticed. Their only hope was that Lady Tremaine would fail to recognize Ona.

Dawn nodded at the guards as she and Ona left the ward, her anxiety barely hidden. There were footsteps from below, more than one set. The warden emerged before them and Dawn smiled, stepping in front of Ona.

"The merchant's son is stable," she said. "We must expand our search to the city—"

"Enough," said the warden. "Do you take me for a fool, girl?" She was flanked by four Guards of the Sun, who blocked the stairs completely. "You," the warden barked at one of her guards, "escort the princess back to her chambers and see that they are properly secured. The rest of you, return the Whisperer to the Spiral Tower. She is to be held there in confinement until such time as the king sees fit."

"You can't do that!" Dawn said. "There is a Narlaw among us. It must be found and banished, I have to—"

"Seize her!" the warden commanded.

Dawn struggled as strong hands took hold of her arms and dragged her towards the stairs. Ona cried out behind her.

"There are no Narlaw here," the warden droned. "Only a saboteur from the out-country who has clearly tried to take his own life with poison."

"That's not true," Dawn shouted. "You're making a mistake. Let me go!"

From the top of the stairs Lady Tremaine sneered down at her. "You broke King Eneron's decree, Whisperer. You were warned to leave the princess alone and yet here you are, arranging secret meetings with a treasonous Southlander."

As Dawn emerged into the courtyard, Ebony swooped down and pecked at the guards, but there were four of them, heavily armoured and strong.

No, Dawn whispered. *You must fly. Don't let them trap you.*

Ebony ascended, out of reach. *Be strong*, she called. *A Whisperer is free even in chains.*

Dawn went quietly with the guards then, watching Ebony soar ahead of her. She feared for Princess Ona, for Yusuf, but most of all for Meridina. The Narlaw were real and they were here among them. This was how it had begun in Queen Amina's time, through sabotage and spying. Next would come the attacks on the borderlands, building and building until the invasion. She had to stop the Narlaw getting any further; she had to make the king and the warden understand before it was too late.

The afternoon faded into dusk. Dawn was brought the usual fine palace food. She called for fresh candles and they were delivered. But while she studied and wrote and puzzled over all of the war histories at her disposal, she was acutely aware of the armed sentries positioned outside her chamber doors.

She was a prisoner – a comfortable one, but a

prisoner nonetheless. The longing she felt to break loose was almost a physical pain. But Ebony had been right: even locked away, Dawn could feel her companion out there in the sky, and through their bond came a version of the soaring freedom of flight.

Ebony carried notes to Captain Valderin, first explaining where Dawn was and then suggesting a widening of the search to encompass the entire city of Meridar. Dawn wished she was out there, but she was stuck, back with her books, while a demon – maybe more than one – stalked the streets of Meridar and perhaps the palace itself.

As night fell, Dawn found herself too exhausted to read any more. The candles on her desk were guttering. Ebony was out, patrolling the skies above the city in hopes of sighting the demon, or picking up its tainted presence.

Dawn sat back in her chair and closed her eyes. She reached out slowly, carefully, with her Whisperer sense, feeling for the living things around her. She had known from an early age how strong she was. This was part of her selection as Palace

Whisperer; a raven companion came only to those of great ability. It was for this reason that Dawn rarely used her full senses, not here in the palace. There were so many people, so many animals, that to reach out fully was overwhelming – a giddy, disconcerting experience.

But now it was all that she wanted, to feel if Ebony was close, to sense what danger lurked in the rooms and corridors around her.

She felt the guards first, silent and stoical, then, as she pushed out further, the residents, maids and soldiers in the rooms below and to the side. She reached further still, down into the courtyard. Birds lingered there, darting free among the fruit trees and the flowerbeds. More guards stood sentry at the base of the tower, two to each entrance.

And then, in the courtyard, something else. A presence she didn't recognize – still and watchful, hidden beneath the dense canopy of trees and shrubs on the far side of the open space.

Dawn opened her eyes, her heart quickening. The sickness spoken of in the old accounts had not come, but what if things were different now? This presence, hiding from the guards, was not human – what if it was a demon?

She rose and dashed from the anteroom to her bedchamber, to the small balcony that overlooked the courtyard. The torches made a flickering pattern of shadow on the walls. Dawn peered into the foliage. She focused on the presence there. A serving man strode across the yard with a stack of trays. The birds twittered in the trees.

Dawn stood motionless in the night air, grasping the rail of the balcony. She reached out, concentrating on that strange presence, forming words in her mind the way Esther had taught her and then expressing those words as pure meaning, as only the strongest of Whisperers could.

She sent the words out: *Show yourself.*

Beneath an apple tree the foliage shifted, so minutely that it could have simply been the breeze. But Dawn felt the visiting presence stir. A pair of eyes glowed suddenly, shrouded in leaves, angled up to meet her gaze.

Torchlight flickered and for an instant she saw the long, grey features of a wolf. There was something lodged between its jaws.

Dawn reached out to the wolf. She could not speak with it, but strongly felt its wariness and its urgent desire to leave this noisy, crowded place. She felt no hostility, and in return projected a wordless message of friendship.

The wolf lowered its muzzle and laid its burden on the ground, under cover of the hanging leaves. It was a courier's tube; Dawn recognized it now. The wolf was a messenger.

It backed into the foliage. Dawn felt its presence slink away through the shadows. How it had made its way so deep into the palace she would never know, only that the creatures of the wild were more skilful than any human could imagine.

She memorized the spot and returned to her study, more eager than ever for Ebony's return.

By midnight the courier tube lay open on Dawn's cluttered desk, its contents unrolled and pinned flat. The message was very troubling indeed.

There were Narlaw in the north. A village had been raided and several citizens taken. The village Whisperers, Moraine and her novice, Alice, requested help from the palace. Just like before, in Queen Amina's time, the Narlaw were trying to take the outlying towns by stealth. And what would come next? A full-scale invasion?

These were terrifying thoughts, but they were a sign that Dawn had to act quickly.

She addressed a note to Valderin, ordering the dispatch of as many guards as he could spare to this northern village. She watched as Ebony carried the message from the tower, her black wings merging with the night. Then, when Ebony was gone, Dawn remained on the balcony, staring blindly at the pitch dark sky.

Already the responsibilities of palace life weighed heavily on her shoulders, but now a new kind of pressure had emerged. History itself had come calling; the hundred-year peace hung in the balance.

Dawn's mind raced with questions: Why now? Why her? Why couldn't Esther be here to help?

But such questions were pointless. They had no answer.

Dawn was the youngest Whisperer the palace had ever known, but still she must do her duty. And her duty was clear.

There was another command that she must dispatch tonight, the likes of which had not been seen since Queen Amina's reign. It was a command bound for every corner of Meridina, and one that could not be written in ink. She would whisper her chosen words to Ebony and Ebony would fly to the deep forest, to the wild ravens who were the agents of the earth itself. Only these wildest of birds could seek out every living Whisperer in the kingdom and pass her message on.

It was a dark message for dark times.

A summons to a council of war.

CHAPTER 9

For Alice, the day passed in a whirl of desperate energy, every thought and movement made sharp by the shock of what had happened in the forest.

Moraine was gone.

And Hazel was gone, too, deep in the forest in desperate pursuit of her companion.

Alice had obeyed Moraine's last wish and escorted the villagers home, she and Owen spreading word of the Narlaw strike. An emergency council meeting had been held, followed by a night of fortification and planning. Gates were reinforced, alleyways blocked. The villagers worked through the night and everybody who could lift a hammer was called into service by the elders; but Alice knew that these defences would not hold for long against a Narlaw attack. She had seen the demons move, witnessed their speed and agility, felt their terrifying strength.

So she had agreed another plan with the village elders: to head out in search of help from Soraya, Moraine's old friend, at Blind Crag.

Alice spent the first dark hours of the night in Moraine's study, searching through her mentor's notes and belongings. Her sense of panic and loss only grew more intense. Loose pages cascaded to the floor and Alice struggled to steady her emotions as she scanned for the information that she needed. At last she found it, scrawled on the reverse side of an inventory of meadow flowers: Soraya and the Blind Crag. The directions were cryptic, intended for Moraine alone, but Alice knew the forest better than anyone. If Soraya could be found, then she would find her.

Outside, Storm was pacing listlessly. Moonlight fell between the trees and tipped her dark fur with flashes of silver.

I've got something, Alice said, waving Moraine's notes. *If we leave at dawn, we may be back here with*

Soraya before nightfall.

If she is still on the mountain, Storm replied. She snorted, agitated, still not herself after tasting the Narlaw flesh.

Alice nodded. There were too many factors yet unknown, too many ways in which they could falter. But one thing Alice did know: she could not banish the Narlaw alone.

They agreed to rest for what remained of the night and Alice curled up in her bed inside the cottage. She slept fitfully. Storm's presence came and went throughout the night and Alice knew that her friend was patrolling, guarding her from what terrors might come at them from the forest. She dreamed of being a wolf, of running fast and free without rest and of howling into the vastness of the scent-filled sky.

At dawn Alice woke to find Storm at her bedside. She trailed a weary hand out of bed and Storm nuzzled in, her breath warm in the chill autumn air.

Side by side, Alice and Storm set off into the forest. The first of Moraine's directions was simple: *north-east to the third ridge*. It was at least an hour's walk from the cottage, so Alice set a brisk pace. Storm loped beside her, distracted and slow. All Alice could do was hope that the poisonous effects would wear off and that her companion would be back to normal soon. She needed Storm, and so did the village.

You were brave yesterday, Alice told her. *Without you the villagers would never have made it to safety.*

Storm snorted, narrowing her eyes. *When the demons are gone from here*, she said. *Only then will anyone be safe.*

Yes, said Alice. She ran her hand softly over her friend's back.

The forest was eerily empty. The trees without birds or insects loomed deathly silent all around them. They went quickly, watching and listening, always ready for the approach of the demons.

They reached the base of the third ridge at mid-morning. A stream meandered through the forest here, bending and looping around the steep contours of land. They followed, against the flow of water until it joined with another stream, one which tumbled noisily over fist-sized rocks.

The second of Moraine's instructions repeated over and over in Alice's head: *Go north where the sage and ironweed grow.*

Alice picked her way upstream, on the hunt for a clearing in the canopy. Sage grew best in the sunlight, and usually away from the wet riverside soil. But this didn't help them much, as ironweed would grow virtually anywhere. All Alice could do was rely on Storm's acute sense of smell.

It wasn't long before Storm paused, sniffing the air.

There, she said, peering across the stream. *Sage.*

She splashed into the stream and Alice followed, drenching her boots in the cool water.

On the other side, Alice pushed her way through a dense wall of foliage. She heard Storm easily winding through ahead of her. Then she emerged into a small clearing, the sun slanting down on to a thick swathe of knee-high sage fronds, scattered throughout with the swaying blue flowers of the ironweed plant. Storm's grey-black neck arched above the plants, proud yet still uneasy.

A path, she said. *North.*

It led uphill, away from the stream and on to the mountain.

For just a moment Alice let the sun settle on her face and breathed in the sage-scented air. Then she strode through the clearing, joining Storm on the northbound trail.

As they climbed higher into the foothills, the earth beneath their feet became stony and dry. Soon the forest thinned to almost nothing. Alice watched the sun approach its peak and felt its warmth on the back of her neck.

Moraine's one remaining instruction referred to a scree slope, and every time Alice squinted up the mountainside she could see it: a bank of loose rock fragments, high and frighteningly steep.

Storm didn't wait for her when they reached the base of the slope, bounding instead over the shards of rock as if it were solid ground.

Wait! Alice called, but Storm was gone.

There was nothing for it. Alice launched herself into the climb.

The scree slid away beneath her boots and at every step she slipped and sank. She dragged herself onwards with her hands, but whenever she stopped for breath she immediately began to slide backwards. The only thing she could do was carry on with the energy-sapping climb.

Slowly Alice ascended. The summit drew closer, a lip of rock that promised some sort of level ground. As she made the final few strides she reached out, but there was a tall step of sheer rock between her and the summit and she struggled to reach the top. Her fingers scraped the ledge and slipped back. Alice scrambled and grabbed hold, but there was no strength left in her arms. She couldn't pull herself up.

Her feet scraped uselessly, sending an avalanche of scree down the slope. She glanced down. It was much higher than she'd thought. If she fell now, she would slide the whole way with nothing to stop her before she crashed into the jagged rocks below.

With one last thrust Alice tried to drag herself on to the ledge, but her muscles failed her. Her fingers were about to give out. She closed her eyes ready for the fall and opened her mouth to cry out. But before any sound escaped her, a shadow appeared above. Storm's teeth flashed and Alice felt herself lifted by the collar of her coat. She grasped at the rock and rolled up on to solid ground, chest heaving, mouth working in silent thanks.

I forget you two-legged beasts are no good at climbing, Storm said.

Alice squinted up at her, still panting. *Thanks*, she said.

They were on a rocky plateau that wound along the crooked mountainside. Below them were the great forested foothills, and several miles away the village could be seen, the bell tower and festival tree standing out against the otherwise unbroken forest canopy. Above them the mountain rose to its craggy, snow-capped peak. It was a dizzying view.

Alice stood and scanned the plateau. It was a place of prickly shrubs, stunted trees and boulders. The mountainside was creased with fissures and openings of all sizes, some dry, some trickling with water.

According to Moraine's notes, Soraya was here somewhere – if she was here at all.

Come on, said Alice. *Let me know if you smell anything interesting.*

Storm padded alongside her, examining these new surroundings with her keen eyes. She seemed more focused now the effects of the Narlaw were wearing off.

Alice let her Whisperer sense wander. She searched the recesses of the mountainside, the scrappy forest on the slopes below, all the while traversing the plateau with the sun now shining powerfully from the south.

They passed into a shaded area, where an

immense rubble of boulders lay piled to twice the height of their cottage. The air became still. Then Storm suddenly stopped, her ears pointed forwards.

Alice peered ahead, probing with all her senses. Beyond the rocks the sun was blinding. She squinted, listening.

Storm's ears twitched.

"Welcome," came a quiet voice from behind them.

Alice spun and stumbled back towards Storm.

Storm growled, leaping to Alice's side.

"No need for alarm," the old woman said. Her sun-baked face creased into a smile. "Come. You must be thirsty."

The woman turned and seemed to vanish between two boulders, down a path so narrow and shadowed that both Alice and Storm had missed it entirely as they had passed.

It's her, whispered Alice.

Yes, Storm replied.

The woman's presence hovered like a ghost in Alice's consciousness.

Alice crept into the fissure and she and Storm trod carefully along a winding path that led up stone steps and over tiny trickling streams. Soon they arrived in a broad cave, into which several large openings spilled light and air, pushing the shadows back a good twenty paces into the mountain. Alice peered into the dark. There was no knowing how far back the cave reached, or what lurked there beneath so many tonnes of rock.

"Sit," Soraya said.

She gestured to a ledge that had been draped with a variety of patterned textiles and laid with wooden cups and a water flask. The cave was furnished like a room in a simple cottage, the walls covered with faded tapestries, a fire pit in pride of place at the centre. There were woven charms hanging all around, like those Moraine made back in the forest. Alice could feel the power and the calm of this place.

As she perched on the ledge, she discreetly studied Soraya – this woman who had lived since the Narlaw Wars, a hundred years before Alice had even been born.

"Come, Storm," Soraya said, gesturing with an open hand. "You should sit, too."

"You know her name?" said Alice, as Storm approached the ledge.

"Of course. Moraine spoke proudly of you both."

Alice nodded, thinking painfully of Moraine. Her restless gaze was drawn towards the darkness at the back of the cave. Did Soraya live here alone? Did she have a companion? Alice could not detect the presence of any other living thing.

She fooled us before, Storm whispered, sensing the direction of Alice's thoughts.

Storm was right. Neither of them had felt Soraya's presence as she had approached them on the mountainside.

The old woman set herself down carefully on an age-flattened rock, and with her small bright eyes she watched Alice take a drink of water. She seemed to be waiting for something.

"Moraine is gone," Alice said. "There are Narlaw in the forest."

Soraya dipped her head in a solitary nod.

"History repeats itself," she muttered thoughtfully. "The wards we set... Well, nothing lasts forever." She looked up to meet Alice's gaze. "So you came to me for help," she said.

"The demons took some villagers, too," said Alice. "I can't banish the Narlaw on my own. Moraine tried to and..."

Her eyes began to sting. She turned away from Soraya, reaching out instinctively to Storm, who nuzzled into her hand. Alice forced back the tears, annoyed with herself. She hadn't come all this way just to cry in front of a stranger.

"I see, child. I see."

"We need your help," Alice said. "If you've banished Narlaw before, you could save the village. And Moraine."

Soraya rose and shuffled slowly into the centre of the sunlit cave. Alice felt a sudden stirring somewhere in the dark, a presence unfelt until now, something huge and old and slowly awakening. Was this Soraya's companion? She wanted badly to know, but didn't dare ask.

"I cannot leave this mountainside," said Soraya. "I am old. Unnaturally so." She turned and narrowed her eyes at the slanting sun. "If I leave I will certainly die. And then my only use is to the wild things who will feed on my body and return me to the bountiful earth."

"But we need you," Alice said.

If she and Storm returned to the village alone then all would be lost. She felt giddy with fear. Moraine had told her to come here, to ask for Soraya's help. Surely all this could not have been for nothing?

"Do not despair, child." Soraya came towards her and pressed her hands to Alice's cheeks. They were cool and unexpectedly smooth. Her eyes shone like black diamonds.

You are a Whisperer.

The words blossomed silently in Alice's mind.

There is nothing you cannot learn.

They sat together on the plateau, Alice and Soraya, in the full glare of the midday sun. Storm was behind them, higher up beside the cave mouth, watching.

"This," Soraya said to Alice. "The forest. The mountain. The wild earth. It is rich with life. You are part of this one living world, and yet, like all beasts, you stand separate from it, too. Separate to observe and to think and act as you please. But few beasts possess the gifts that you do – or the depth of responsibility. Only a Whisperer may consciously commune with the earth. Only a Whisperer can sense the living things around her without use of sight or sound. And only a Whisperer can banish a demon to the Darklands. We are the guardians of it all, my child.

"You have been trained well by Moraine. She is strong and learned and she cares a great deal for the people of the mountain and for the forest itself. But you and she are very different."

"I can't concentrate like she can," Alice said. "The earth trance… I almost held it yesterday, but it slipped away from me like it always does. If I can't do that, how can I learn to banish the Narlaw?" Soraya smiled, her legs dangling from the rock she had perched upon, and Alice thought how childlike the ancient Whisperer was.

"There is more than one way to banish a demon," Soraya said. "You must choose the way that is closest to your nature."

Alice stared out over the vast forest. "My nature?"

"For you, the forest is never silent. You cannot block it from your mind and you refuse to relinquish your bond with Storm, not even for the purposes of the earth trance."

"Is that what Moraine told you?"

Soraya shook her head. "It is what your presence here has told me."

"So what should I do?"

"Where some would silence the world, you must reach out and open your senses to everything – the trees, the air, the insects and the birds, the tiny creeping things. You must hold on to Storm. And then you must go further. Embrace all that you can and the earth will join with you."

"And the Narlaw?"

"The Narlaw will be a part of that embrace."

Alice shivered as she remembered the foul, sickening presence. Reach out to the Narlaw? How could she manage such a thing?

"In a time of strife, there is no easy way," Soraya said. "I was only a fraction older than you when the Narlaw came. I thought myself unready, unable to fight. But, like you, I was already a Whisperer. I had no choice but to play my part."

She placed a gentle hand on Alice's back.

"Will you try with me? There are no demons here. You have nothing to fear."

As the afternoon came and the sun scrolled across the sky, Alice sat above the great forest and tried to gather in the world.

Soraya whispered to her. *Reach further, child. Feel for the treetops, touch the stones in the riverbed.*

Alice pushed her senses as far as she could, and each time she thought she had reached her limit, Soraya found a way to stretch them further. The whole valley hovered within her grasp; every living thing was there. She felt the river water rushing over rocks and the air press against the wings of birds. She felt the creeping, skittering beasts of the forest like a shifting constellation of souls. She felt Soraya beside her and Storm above her on the spur of rock. And deep within the mountain she felt that other thing, the ancient presence freshly woken from its slumber.

She practised until her casting of this vast net was automatic, and swift as an adder's strike. It was a rush of feeling like nothing she had known – more overwhelming, even, than the calm intensity of the earth trance.

You have embraced the living valley, Soraya whispered to her. *The earth feels you. You have shown it this valley like an offering.*

But there are no Narlaw here, Alice whispered.

No, Soraya replied. *That is a challenge you are yet to face.*

Alone.

Only a Whisperer can gather in the demons. You are the channel – the earth will act through you. If you are steadfast and fearless then it will banish them.

Alice let the valley go. The feeling rushed away and she sat experiencing the light and air and the rock beneath her through her five simple senses.

"You see now that you have strength," said Soraya. "But you will need yet more. The demons slide through this world like quicksilver and will do everything to evade your touch. The chaos of battle will confuse things."

"I wish you could come with me," Alice said.

Soraya smiled. "So do I." She glanced back at her mountain home. "But I must stay."

They ate a small meal together at the entrance to the cave – a sweet-tasting root and shreds of raw rabbit for Storm. Alice sensed her friend's anxiety, the restless desire to act that matched her own. In a few hours dusk would come and the village would be so much more vulnerable.

"We should go now," she said to Soraya. "Thank you for the food. And for … everything."

Soraya inclined her head. "Do what must be

done," she said. Her eyes glittered, steely and bright.

Alice nodded. "I'll try."

Soraya took them to a secluded path that skirted the scree slope. Storm went ahead and Alice next, seizing her chance to ask the question that had been troubling her since their arrival at Blind Crag.

"Your companion," she said. "Why does she hide from us?"

Soraya was silent for a moment behind her.

"There are so few Whisperers now," she said. "Especially here at the edge of the kingdom. Do you know how I grew so old, child?"

Alice shook her head.

"My companion and I have a way of sharing our time here. One sleeps while the other watches. It is an old skill, not much used, but it has allowed us a great deal more life than is normal. This is also the reason why I cannot leave my home. Our link is different to the one you have with Storm. To separate would bring the risk of death to us both."

"It felt as if your companion was waking," said Alice. "Back in the cave."

"Yes," said Soraya. "And now it is my turn to sleep. Perhaps for the last time."

"What do you mean?" said Alice.

She turned sharply, but Soraya was already gone. Gone too was her calm and powerful presence, as abruptly as it had appeared that morning.

CHAPTER 10

They made good time back through the valley, Storm trotting a few paces ahead with her ears twitching and her nose sniffing the air.

It was a relief for Alice to see that Storm seemed fully recovered – Alice needed her by her side tonight, ready to do battle.

The techniques she had learned from Soraya had boosted her confidence, but they had brought new fears, too. Alice knew she could cast her senses wide, that she could embrace vast tracts of the forest, but with the Narlaw in among them everything would be different. She had no idea how the Narlaw's touch would feel, or how she might react. No matter what Soraya had said, she was heading into the unknown and into danger.

They continued into the forest. The sky had clouded over since they had left the mountain and a dimness had settled between the trees. Alice watched as Storm bounded ahead, nose raised to the air.

No, she said. *No, no, no.* She darted in another direction, still sniffing.

What is it? Alice asked, running to her side.

Fire! said Storm.

That single word sent a bolt of fear through Alice's body and she ran beside Storm with a deadly panic inside her. She had heard tales of bush fires, down in the arid south of Meridina, terrible blazes that burned for days on end and consumed whole towns, whole stretches of the wild. But here in the north, they were unheard of. There was too much rain and moisture. It simply didn't happen.

In just a few moments, though, Alice saw that Storm was right.

First came the smoke. It drifted through the trees, stinging Alice's eyes and burning her throat. Then came the crackling, popping, creaking cacophony of the blaze. And slowly, building and building, came the heat.

Alice stopped beside Storm as the smoke-shrouded flames flickered into view. Even at a distance the heat was intense. Alice raised a hand to shield her face and Storm darted left, becoming just a dark grey smudge in the blanket of smoke.

Stay close! Alice shouted.

Storm came back to her. *We must find a way around.*

I know, said Alice. *We'll be cut off from the village.*

Somewhere in the midst of the blaze, a tree creaked and fell. A wave of hot air rushed out and Alice turned her back to the flames, retreating from the blast. Her eyes watered painfully and even with her hand across her mouth she tasted the hot, choking smoke with every breath.

There has to be a way! said Storm.

Wait, said Alice. *I'm thinking.*

If we don't go now, we'll be trapped. We have to get help from the village!

Alice stumbled further from the blaze. She knew

how quickly a fire could spread, and how deadly the smoke and the heat were. What was more, the fire seemed to be spreading down the mountainside – straight towards their cottage and the village. They had to stop it. Alice thought back to her training; there was something Moraine had taught her, long ago, something powerful…

A dousing ward! she cried, the words collapsing into a painful cough as she spoke.

We don't have time for that, said Storm.

It's all we have time for, Alice said. *The fire will be too large to tackle by the time we reach the village. We have to try and stop it now. Come. Help me. We need fireweed blossom, arnica and … and dog lichen!*

She ran away from the blaze until gradually the smoke thinned and she could see the forest floor again.

Dog lichen loves the knots of old oaks, she said. *I'll look for that. You sniff for the arnica and fireweed.*

Storm darted off with her nose to the ground and Alice ran in search of an oak amidst the pines. They were sparse at this altitude, but there had to be one at least.

A few seconds later Storm raised a brief howl and Alice ran to her.

Fireweed, Storm said, before rushing off to hunt for the arnica.

Alice bent and picked a handful of the shrub's lilac blossoms, stuffing the petals into her jacket pocket. She looked up. There between the arrow-straight pines stood a small, twisted oak. She hurried over and examined the bark, coughing from the drifting shreds of smoke as she circled the tree. There. One tiny green sprouting of dog lichen on the outside of an eye-shaped knot. She scraped it off with her thumbnail and added it to the fireweed in her pocket. She turned and, through the smoke, Storm appeared, a bright yellow spray of arnica flowers in her mouth.

"That's everything," Alice said, breathing as shallowly as she could.

She took the arnica and found herself a large flat rock and a fist-sized pebble with which to grind the ingredients together.

The dousing ward was meant for small fires –

a stove or a cottage roof, even. Strictly you were meant to scatter the mixture around the circumference of the blaze. But that was impossible here. There wasn't enough lichen in the entire forest for that. No. Alice had a different plan. If she could ignite the mixture near the centre of the blaze then, instead of eating the fire from the outside, it might, just might, work the other way, expanding from the epicentre, dousing the blaze from within.

When she told Storm they had to reach the centre of the fire, Storm didn't object. She had noticed the same thing Alice had: the stream – the tiny river they had followed to find Soraya – it flowed directly into the blaze. Alice folded the mixture away in a scrap of cloth and they set off.

Storm easily located the stream and Alice splashed in behind her. As they ran towards the heart of the fire, Alice found herself wishing she had four legs not two, so she could run low and fast below the choking, billowing smoke.

The forest burned around them. Trees splintered and fell out of sight, sap boiled and hissed, and pine needles sparked, disintegrating into ash on the forest floor. The heat was almost unbearable. Alice slid off her belt sash and moistened it, wrapping it around her nose and mouth as she swept downstream behind Storm. The smoke rolled over her. Storm flashed in and out of sight a few paces ahead.

Just then a hideous noise split the air. Alice looked up. A giant pine lurched, branches swaying, and sheared off at the bottom of the trunk.

Storm! Alice cried.

Storm leaped forward as the huge tree crashed across the stream, throwing up water, earth and flame where Storm had been a moment before.

Alice stumbled backwards, covering her eyes. Branches burned and sparked all around. The river was blocked.

Storm! she called again.

But the noise was deafening. She reached out with all her senses and felt her companion instantly.

Go under, Storm said. *Quickly.*

Alice glanced through her raised hand at the fallen tree. The stream hissed as burning pine needles fell. The heat was incredible.

You can do it, Storm said.

Alice took a long, burning breath and plunged below the water line.

The stream was only waist deep, but that was enough. She peered through the churning water, saw the trunk dipping inches under the surface as if it were floating. There was room, but only just. She kicked out with her legs and scrambled along the pebbly river bed. The trunk scraped her head and she lost her handhold, floating up towards the blazing heat. Her lungs ached, already scorched from the smoke and now desperate for air of any kind. She twisted on to her back and used the trunk to propel herself forward. She surfaced under a burning branch and felt the flames singe her hair before she managed to duck back under. Seconds later she was clear, rising to her feet, water rushing down her face and the choking hot air flowing back into her lungs.

She stumbled, but Storm held her steady.

Alice coughed and spat water. A circle of ash

and blackened trees spread out around her with the stream at its centre.

Here, she said.

Storm helped her to the nearest bank, up on to the dead patch of forest and across the scorched ground towards the flames. The river water helped against the searing heat, but she felt it burning away even as she stood.

She took the damp parcel from her inside pocket and unfolded it with shaking hands. The words came back to her. She heard Moraine's calm, thoughtful voice as she spoke them, scattering the mixture into the fire. A green flame shot up from the ground. It was cool, instantly shielding her from the burning trees. Alice chanted, calling to the earth, whispering to the life-giving soil. She stepped carefully around the inner circle of fire, casting tiny pinches of the mixture and calling up the green dousing flame, completing the circle.

The new fire leaped up, consuming the orange flames and making the air inside the circle breathable again. It was working. The dousing fire spread into the forest, tree to tree, leaving the earth to quietly smoulder in its wake.

Alice collapsed on to the riverbank, utterly exhausted. Minutes later an eerie silence fell. Only the tumbling of the stream could be heard. The forest fire was extinguished.

Storm prowled across the bed of ash, the epicentre of the fire. She nosed into the charred black flakes, the fallen branches.

There is a scent underneath, she said. *Before the fire came demons.*

Alice looked up. *Are you sure?*

They started this, said Storm. *There are trails. I know the taste now.*

Alice rose to her feet. Her body ached. Her chest stung as she inhaled. So the Narlaw had tried to destroy the forest, to isolate the villagers.

We have to go, she said.

Yes, said Storm. *They mean to take the village. Soon.*

Alice nodded. Tonight then. She would attempt what had not been done in a hundred years: a banishment of demons.

CHAPTER 11

The sun was already low in the sky when Alice and Storm approached the village. The palisade walls stood tall, still woven with the star-flowered stems of the protective ward, and the ward itself reappeared as a shining ring at the edge of Alice's consciousness.

A small group of villagers clustered around the north gate. They carried pails of water and looked tired and smoke-sick. They turned and grew silent as Alice and Storm emerged form the trees.

"Did you find her?" called Elder Garth, separating from the group. "The ancient one. Where is she?"

"She couldn't come," said Alice, crossing the clearing with Storm at her side.

"But the fire," Garth stuttered. "It … it vanished.

There was magic done…"

Alice strode past him towards the open north gate. "Not magic – Whisperer craft. An old trick Moraine taught me."

A ripple of surprise spread through the group and, for the first time, Alice caught on the faces of the villagers not scorn or distaste, but a fearful respect.

The streets had been transformed. Blockades had been built, patchwork walls made of timber that reached to the roofs of the cottages. The people had completely altered their homes for the good of the village and that made her think of her own home. Although they had doused the forest fire, the cottage she shared with Moraine would have been badly damaged. It angered her more than ever that these demons could come into her forest and destroy everything in their path.

Alice continued through the village. She turned sharply, following the route the barricades forced her to take. She arrived at a particularly narrow alleyway. It looked clear, but as she and Storm headed through towards the market square a voice called out and a hand appeared on her shoulder.

"Wait! The trap is primed!"

Alice stopped and found the apprentice boy, Owen, beside her.

"What do you mean?" she said.

Storm had stopped a pace ahead, sniffing at the muddy ground.

"It's a hunting channel," Owen said. "They use them to trap fast-moving animals in the forest. Stand back," he said. "I'll show you."

Alice stepped into an open doorway and Storm followed her in with narrowed eyes. Owen squeezed past them into the cottage and came back out with a small barrel in his arms.

"Watch," he said.

He carried the barrel back the way Alice and Storm had come, then he turned and hurled it down the alley. As it bounced through the mud beyond the doorway there was a loud click, and from the outer wall of the cottage swung a huge net set in a wooden frame. The net was more than two paces square and it was swift and powerful. It crashed into the wall of the cottage at the end of its arc, pinning the barrel against the wall. Owen ran and quickly wound a rope to secure the net to the cottage wall. The barrel was trapped.

Alice turned to him, impressed. "You made this?" she asked.

Owen nodded. "I'm a carpenter. Apprentice actually, but … well … the Narlaw took my father, so I'm in charge of his workshop for now."

"It's incredible," Alice said.

Owen shrugged. "Just a footboard under the mud, a catch and some heavy-duty springs. There's one near the south gate, too, but that was all I could build in time." He cast a troubled look over towards the forest. "I've seen them move," he said. "The demons. They're so strong and fast. I thought trapping them might give us a chance. Give *you* a chance, I mean…"

Alice nodded. No matter how clever and brave the villagers were, no matter how long they fought against the Narlaw, it would always come down to her.

You can do it, Storm said. *You* will *do it*.

Alice laid a hand on Storm's warm, soft back. "We should go to the hall," she said. "I have a ward to set."

In the emergency council meeting she and the elders had drawn up a defence plan. Those who felt willing and able to fight would take up positions around the village, slowing the Narlaw down, trying their best to confuse and blind them with lanterns and burning torches – and now, it seemed, funnelling them towards Owen's traps. The rest of the villagers would stay in the hall, around which Alice would raise a protective ward – smaller and stronger than the one surrounding the village. She had no idea whether it would keep the Narlaw out, but it was the best she could do.

As she and Storm crossed the market square it was clear that word of their arrival had already reached the village hall. Several elders came to meet her at the bottom of the steps.

"It seems we have you to thank for extinguishing the forest fire?" Elder Byrne said. She was a school teacher and had something of Moraine's gentle authority about her. She smiled, though her face was tight with worry. "We have gathered people inside," she said. "Come. Tell us what you need."

Alice had arranged for certain of Moraine's protective compounds to be brought here while she was searching for Soraya. And that was her first task: to set a strong ward around this building, something that would hold the Narlaw at bay and give her a chance to attempt the banishment. As she climbed the steps towards the hall, Alice realized Storm was not following her. She turned.

I will call again for the wolf packs, Storm said. *They fear the Narlaw more than ever now, but perhaps some will join us in this fight.*

Thank you, whispered Alice.

She watched as Storm trotted swiftly across the square and out of sight, hoping that her friend would not be gone long. The thought of what might happen that night – of what she had to do – weighed heavily on her. Her stomach fluttered with nerves and she clenched her fists to keep her hands from shaking.

Alice followed Elder Byrne into the village hall, into the murmuring mass of people; a hundred heads turned and all eyes fixed on her. Every gaze was charged with the desperate, terrified need for protection.

Evening came. The ward was set.

Alice stood in the bell tower scanning the forest canopy – the forest that had been her home for as long as she could remember, and that now was the domain of demons.

The fire had left a scar on the mountainside much larger than she had imagined, making clear what might have been. The Narlaw truly were destroyers of life. If they were not stopped here, these few would spread from village to village, town to town, laying waste to the great forest. More Narlaw would creep across the passes from the Darklands, sinking more and more people into the ghost-sleep until all the north was in their grasp.

Alice stared into the deep green, the swaying treetops burnished gold by the setting sun. Moraine was out there, too. And the village hunters. They would sleep forever if the banishment failed, if Alice could not save them. She practised casting out with her Whisperer sense; casting out and then withdrawing a little further each time, as Soraya had taught her. There was no sign yet of the Narlaw's slick, unnatural presence – nor of help from the palace.

The villagers were as restless as ants in the hall below, and the brave souls out in the village were dug in to their defensive positions, awaiting the onset of night and the coming battle. Alice sensed each living presence, some pulsing with fear, some strangely calm. She felt fear herself, like a cold stone in her stomach, but all the living beings around her gave her strength; none more so than the warm, familiar presence that climbed towards her up the stairs of the bell tower.

Storm appeared through the opening in the floor, her fur immediately ruffled by the wind and her golden eyes shining in the half light. Alice smiled and stepped away from the parapet. It was cold and a long night was coming. But Storm was with her, which meant that anything was possible.

CHAPTER 12

Far below Dawn, the streets of Meridar glowed as if they were the embers of some great campfire. From her balcony in the Spiral Tower, she watched the streetlamps flicker. She heard the distant cry of the night watchman and smelled the faint tang of chimney smoke. Small flocks of birds flickered across the moonlit sky, the birds Ebony had coaxed into the search for the Narlaw spy. One by one they had landed at the infirmary window to view the sleeping form of the merchant's son, then flown off into the city skies to hunt for Yusuf's demon counterpart.

Dawn leaned into the breeze. Even in calm weather, the wind up here on the tower was enough to fling her hair back like a streamer.

Somewhere in this city was the demon and it was her job to find it, no matter what Lady Tremaine claimed. She left the balcony and stepped down into the relative warmth of her study. The messages sent from Valderin were piled on her desk beside a huge map of the city. Ebony had played messenger all night, and not without complaint.

You should have had a pigeon for a companion, not a raven, she had said.

Dawn smiled. She was awaiting the response from one last message. Not from Valderin, but Princess Ona.

There was a heavy thump against the door and Dawn started. It was time.

"Enter," she called.

The door swung open and one of the red-draped Guards of the Sun stepped inside, ushering in a kitchen maid who carried a tray of tea and bread and was heavily wrapped against the night's cold.

Dawn nodded to the guard.

"Thank you," she said to the maid, indicating a space on the edge of the huge desk.

The maid set down her tray and began the laborious process of unwrapping the bread along with a plate and a wedge of cheese. The guard stepped back into the corridor with a look of severe boredom on his blunt features.

As soon as the door closed the maid looked up at Dawn. "We don't have much time," she said in a low voice.

Dawn nodded and removed her Whisperer's robe as the maid did the same with her cloak. They swapped and Dawn noted with satisfaction the maid's long, black hair, near identical to her own. In seconds they had changed places, Dawn standing over the now empty tray and the maid in a chair at the desk, face lowered over the map and documents there.

Dawn took up the tray and, with a whispered thank you, she headed for the door. The maid nodded in response. Dawn didn't know her name – a stern, thoughtful girl. She had simply asked Ona to send someone who might act as a double, and Ona had chosen well.

The guard barely even glanced up as Dawn exited her chambers and she felt a rush of excitement as she strode away towards the servants' stairs. There were two more sets of guards before she was safely out of the tower. With her eyes lowered and a confident, purposeful gait, she made it. She had outwitted Lady Tremaine. Now, though, the real challenge was upon her.

Dawn met Valderin at the edge of the parade ground close to the base of the Spiral Tower. At first glance he seemed to have come alone, but she noticed other individuals idling in the shadows. Neither Valderin nor the others were in uniform.

"You brought some friends," Dawn said.

"In case we had to liberate you from the tower by force," replied Valderin.

"Thank you," said Dawn. "I am quite capable of liberating myself."

Valderin tilted his head in deference. "Of course. The hunt for the demon has progressed more quickly than we expected. Your skills are needed right away."

"You've found the Narlaw?" Dawn inhaled a rapid lungful of the cold night air.

"Yusuf's double was sighted near the docklands one hour ago. We have people patrolling both sides of the river, but there are many hiding places."

"Have you seen Ebony?" Dawn asked.

"Not since your last message," said Valderin.

They approached the main barracks of the palace guards – Valderin's territory. Dawn peered up into the night sky. It looked different from ground level, muddied by lamp light, interrupted by so many jagged rooftops. She called out silently to Ebony, casting her senses skyward, out over the city in gentle waves. The sleeping and the sleepless, the skulking, toiling people of the city flashed into her mind's eye as she did so. She withdrew and cast out again.

Then came the response she desired.

Dawn.

She felt Ebony swooping closer, heard the long,

soft patter of her wings, and then the air eddied and Ebony was with her, talons gently shuffling on her cloaked shoulder.

So you dug your way out? she said.

Something like that, Dawn replied. *There's been a sighting at the docklands.*

Well then. Ebony hopped from one shoulder to the other, stretching her wings. *I'll meet you there. And I'll bring my eyes in the sky.* She cawed and took flight, vanishing into the dark.

Dawn followed Valderin through the guardhouse and out into a small yard where a coach and horses stood waiting. The animals stamped their hooves, snorting impatiently. Dawn felt anxiety radiate from them, something she understood all too well. The city felt strange tonight: birdsong at the wrong hour, all of this secrecy and haste – and a demon. A hundred years had passed since the Narlaw had dared set foot on the soil of Meridina. But now they were back, and it was Dawn's watch. It was she who would have to fight them.

She climbed into the coach along with Valderin

and one of his guards, and was accelerated away into the tangled, troubled streets of the city.

The docklands spanned two sprawling regions on either side of the river. Barges crowded the shores, so numerous sometimes that it seemed as though you could walk from one side of the river to the other across their decks. Private, guarded piers held the yachts of the wealthy and the fleets of trade vessels that carried all kinds of goods in and out of the city. Warehouses, taverns and customs offices lined the riversides like crooked teeth. By day it was a place for traders; by night a place for thieves and smugglers.

The coach rattled into the heart of the Eastern Docks. This was where the Narlaw had been spotted, still in the guise of the young man, Yusuf. Dawn closed her eyes to the shadowy world that flashed by her. She set her Whisperer sense free and reached out for the fugitive demon.

It was the birds who guided her.

At a bend in the river they had gathered, circling. Gulls, crows, sparrows, finches, pigeons – every type of bird. In the midst of that maelstrom of wheeling, darting bodies, Dawn recognized Ebony, too.

"Up ahead!" Dawn called to Valderin, to the coach driver, to anyone.

"Where?" said Valderin. "Do you see the creature?"

"Follow the birds," she said. "Quickly!"

The coach thundered ahead, tilting on its wheels, and Dawn struggled to maintain her vision. With her eyes closed, the movements of the coach were especially sickening and she held fast to a leather strap attached to the door. They swerved around a corner and a group of men yelled angrily at them. The birds thickened into what seemed like a solid mass as they neared the river bend.

"Where now?" Valderin asked.

Dawn scanned the dark buildings of the river front: empty warehouses, lone figures on the street. Then her senses lit with the presence of people. Two taverns, almost side by side. One was packed with revellers, the other quiet, but it had rooms upstairs. The throng of birds was overwhelming and Dawn drew her senses in, concentrating on those taverns. She felt the Narlaw then – a sickly thing, like a knot in her throat. She flinched away.

"The second tavern," she said to Valderin. "Upstairs. In the back corner room, I think."

She opened her eyes and gladly let her senses retract. Valderin was sitting forward in his seat, one hand on his sword hilt and staring out with a serious, fixed expression at the approaching inn.

"Stop here," he ordered the driver.

The horses clattered to a standstill.

"Fetch the others from the rendezvous," Valderin said to the guard who had ridden with them.

The man jumped from the coach and sprinted into the shadows beside the first tavern.

"You should wait here," Valderin said.

Dawn shook her head, despite the fear that was screaming at her to stay in the coach. "You'll need my help," she said.

Valderin narrowed his eyes. He peered out into

the street. Now, with a battle coming, Dawn could see he was a warlike man. His body was coiled and ready.

"As you wish," he said at last. "But let us go in first."

Dawn nodded. She sensed Ebony approaching and twisted as her companion's wings filled the small coach window.

You found it, Ebony said.

Thanks to you and your friends up there, Dawn whispered. *How did they do it?*

Ebony stretched her neck this way and that. *All animals know when something's wrong,* she said. *Pigeons, wrens, starlings … they can feel the Narlaw too, just not as keenly as a Whisperer. The difficult part was convincing them to flock to the source rather than away from it, but that's where being a palace raven comes in useful. Even city birds respect a raven.*

Dawn smiled. *I knew you were good for something.*

Ebony hopped and craned her neck as boots echoed on the cobbles nearby. Several shadows broke from the deeper dark of an alleyway. Valderin's guards, six of them and all in plain clothes.

Valderin climbed from the coach.

Stay close, Dawn said to Ebony as she followed Valderin on to the street.

Always, said Ebony.

"The demon is in the Cross Keys Inn," Valderin was saying to his guards, pointing to the second of the two taverns. "Upstairs at the back. Sergeant, take two people and locate the rear entrances. Wait downstairs until you hear my signal. The rest of you come with me and Dawn. We'll take the direct route."

The sergeant nodded and her long grey hair swayed in its ponytail. She led her team back into the shadows. Dawn strode alongside Valderin, past the crowded inn and its raucous laughter, on to the gloomy, candlelit entrance of the Cross Keys.

Inside was only the barman and one patron, an elderly man who was staring vacantly into his pewter drinking mug. The barman straightened as if he had guessed right away that these new arrivals were not customers, and Valderin began questioning him about the number and location of the rooms upstairs.

Dawn edged between the stained and ill-matching tables and chairs. She could feel the Narlaw now without even reaching out. It hovered over her head like an evil thought. Could it feel her too? She silently rehearsed all of the close-range wards that she knew.

Upstairs the demon's presence shifted.

Dawn glanced at the bar. "Valderin," she said.

Her gaze flashed upwards and he read her meaning. He crossed the room immediately.

"This way," he said.

Dawn followed. The three palace guards raced past her to join their captain. As they rushed through a dim corridor towards an even dimmer stairwell, Valderin whistled once and his sergeant emerged from the rear of the building.

"Wait here," Valderin said. "Don't let the demon escape."

Dawn climbed the stairs, looking back once at the fierce woman guarding the stairs with her sword drawn. "Left," she whispered, reaching the landing.

Valderin led his guards towards the furthest door.

Dawn swallowed down her nausea and fear together. The Narlaw was so close now, she could feel it in her gut.

Valderin stopped at the door. For a moment there was silence, and Dawn could hear her own racing heartbeat. Then Valderin turned to his guards, nodded three times and kicked the door in with a splintering crack.

The next few seconds passed in a frenzied blur.

Dawn ran to the doorway. Two guards were on the floor, a table was overturned and Valderin and the remaining guard were grappling with something that moved much too quickly to be human. Eerie grey light shone from the demon Yusuf's eyes. His limbs twisted, lashing out viciously. He kicked against the wall and sent himself and his two attackers flying across the room.

Valderin hit his head and went down. The last guard stood, terrified by this unearthly creature. The Narlaw glared at Dawn, pure malevolence burning on its stolen features. Then it turned to face the window at the end of the room.

Dawn instinctively began to chant.

The words came as naturally as breath, long practised with Esther. The power flowed through her, from the earth beneath the cobbles, from the surging river and the trembling of the wooden floor. She reached out to the edges of this grimy little room and focused.

The Narlaw leaped for the mottled glass of the window. The wooden frame was mouldy and weak, but Dawn sent her words out like arrows, strengthening the ward.

The Narlaw crashed into the glass with a howl of pain and surprise as the ward held. The demon scrambled to its feet, rounding on Dawn as she stood there, entranced by the power channelling through her. The room was a cage now and she was in it.

As the demon came for her she clenched her teeth and made her last command, her last breathless request to the great earth.

The ward contracted, snapping inwards towards the evil in its midst.

Dawn stumbled back as the demon charged.

Her back hit the wall and she fell to her knees. The demon sprung for her with arms outstretched. She closed her eyes.

But the blow never fell.

The ward closed and the demon was caught in mid-air, its eyes glowing wide with hatred, just half a stride away from Dawn.

The sergeant thundered into the room then and stopped dead at the sight.

Dawn clambered to her feet. "The others," she said, barely able to breathe. "They need help."

The sergeant stared at her in shock, then called downstairs for help before attending to the wounded guards.

The ward crackled and hissed as the demon struggled. It took all of Dawn's strength to hold it in place, but she stood and chanted silently, staring into those ghost-grey eyes, not quite able to believe what she had done.

CHAPTER 13

Alice kept watch from the bell tower as stars blossomed in the sky and the forest heaved like a dark ocean all around. More and more she caught herself glancing south towards the Meridar road, hoping for some sign that their call for help had been answered by the palace. But no soldiers came. The village of Catchwood was alone on the mountainside.

Storm paced behind her, lit by the flickering yellow of a single oil lamp. The hours crept by.

Alice practised her casting out. She shivered from the cold wind and with the nerves that knotted the muscles in her stomach. Still there was no sign of the Narlaw. Perhaps they would not come. Perhaps they had fled. But these were cowardly thoughts and Alice knew it. Wherever the demons were they had to be found and banished, otherwise Moraine and the others would languish forever in the ghost-sleep.

And so the night crawled on. Weariness settled over Alice, threatening to lower her into a guilty sleep. She paced alongside Storm, trying to keep her senses sharp, battling the exhaustion.

Then the moment came: in the dead, dark hours, when the night was at its thickest, the protective ward around the village was breached.

Alice felt it like the crack of a whip inside her head. She cried out, wordlessly.

Storm came to her. *It is time?* she asked.

Alice nodded. *The ward is broken.*

A shout went up in the village, somewhere near the south gate.

Alice glanced once across the dark rooftops then ran to the stairs.

"Sound the bell!" she shouted down. "They're here!"

She looked back at Storm, a fresh panic fluttering

in her chest. The bell clanged furiously below, sending shockwaves through the wooden floor.

Now, said Storm. *You know you can do it.*

Alice nodded, took a deep, deep breath and strode back to the parapet.

Immediately she knew the Narlaw were near. There was a taint in the air, dulled slightly by the ward around the village hall, but sickening nonetheless. Alice cast her senses wide.

The forest felt different at night – different creatures, different movements; even the trees were changed. She felt the gathered people in the hall below and the defenders by the wall, the wolves prowling unseen in the narrow streets and...

The touch of the demon shocked Alice out of her trance. She flinched back from the parapet. It had flashed into her consciousness, lightning quick and brimming with malevolence, like a ghost passing through her body.

So this was how it felt.

Alice shuddered. Six village hunters had been taken by the Narlaw, which meant there were at least five more of these creatures out there. How could she hope to banish them all when she couldn't bare the touch of just one?

The screech and crash of timber split the sky. More shouts went up – the howl of a wolf this time, too. The fighting had begun.

Storm tensed beside her. *I should go*, she said. *The wolves came at my request. I must fight beside them.*

You're right, said Alice, afraid all over again to be left alone on the roof of the tower.

Remember Soraya, said Storm. *You are a Whisperer. You were born to do this.* She rubbed her neck against Alice's side before darting on to the downward stairway.

Alice turned back to the parapet. The sounds of fighting echoed from all corners of the village now. Torchlight flashed between the rooftops. She had to act fast, before they were overrun by the Narlaw. With an effort, Alice closed her eyes to the growing chaos below. She let her Whisperer sense expand and wander, ready this time for the foul touch of the demons. She pushed out to the village wall and beyond, encompassing all of the fear and panic and anger of the siege.

She felt the Narlaw dart and slide across her senses. They moved so quickly, impossible to pin down, always slipping away from her. It seemed deliberate – they were evading her touch. Out in the village someone wailed and then went silent. There was a crash and a sudden panicked shout that brought Alice out of her trance.

"Here! Here!"

It was Owen.

Alice ran to the north-facing edge of the tower and saw a lamp-lit alley flickering with shadows. Several defenders, including Owen, stood uncertainly, staring at the sprung trap from a safe distance.

They had one. They had trapped a Narlaw.

Alice peered down at the thrashing, grey-eyed demon. It was in the form of a young woman from the missing hunting party. Now was Alice's chance.

Alice focused on that one alleyway alone.

There was Owen standing, excited and afraid, with two others. And next to them, pinned to the wall, was the snarling, desperate presence of the Narlaw. Alice let her senses swallow the four of them, the wooden cottages and the dirt beneath their feet. She felt the air brush through Owen's hair, the tiny vibrations in the earth made by the movements of his booted companions. She felt the thrashing, mad, un-breathing Narlaw like a poison inside her.

And she gave herself to the earth.

She held tight to the demon's presence and began to lose herself in the trance. Her body was gone. She floated free with all the particles and currents of the air. And the power of the earth rushed through her, blanking everything.

When her vision and feeling returned she found herself kneeling at the parapet. She rose, her head dizzy and buzzing.

"You did it!" Owen shouted. "It's gone!"

Alice steadied herself, shocked.

She had done it.

She had banished a Narlaw.

But before Alice could respond to Owen there was a terrible splintering noise behind her. She spun around and, out across the rooftops, she saw the south gate fall, taking a long section of the palisade wall with it. Those who had defended it fled towards the heart of the village and, close behind them, with that startling, inhuman speed, came the Narlaw. There were too many to count at once. Ten, fifteen, perhaps. Certainly more than the five Alice had expected. Most were in human form, too distant and too quick to recognize individually. Some came snarling into the village in the guise of wolves.

The villagers ran and Alice saw Storm's wolves darting through the shadows, harrying the demons but incapable even of slowing them down. There were screams, cries of desperation. Alice cast her senses out across the village and recoiled immediately at the seething, chaotic movements of this new band of demons. They were everywhere. She had no chance of holding them long enough to perform the banishment.

Then it struck her. She knew what she must do.

As she charged down the steps of the bell tower she felt the ward around the building tremble. The Narlaw were testing it, trying to get in. Alice reached the main hall and the mass of panic-ridden villagers. The great doors rumbled, a noise strangely deadened by the protective power of the ward and somehow all the more frightening for it.

"Where are you going?" asked Elder Garth. "You can't leave us!"

"This is the only way," Alice said, surprised at the calmness of her voice.

She reached the doors and the squad of armed guards turned to face her.

"Open them," Alice said. "The ward will hold. They cannot pass. Not yet."

"But…" stuttered a large man holding a makeshift pike.

"Just do it," Alice ordered. "I cannot do my work from inside."

The guards unbolted the doors and, after an exchange of worried glances, flung them open, ready with their weapons. The steps were empty but Alice probed ahead. Perhaps the Narlaw were afraid of her. They must know by now that she had banished one of their kind. She peered out into the village square. The festival tree towered over a scene of eerie calm. The air clamoured with the sounds of battle, but the open square lay empty.

Alice passed through the ward and felt it shimmer over her. She stepped down into the pure clarity of the outside. The doors slammed shut behind her and she was alone once more.

She closed her eyes and reached out to Storm. *Come to me,* she whispered.

Storm howled into the night sky and the thundering of paws echoed from the western streets of the village. Alice strode to the shelter of the festival tree and in seconds Storm was at her side, with a pack of eight tough-looking wolves behind her.

Why did you leave the tower? asked Storm. She was breathing heavily.

I need the demons close to me, all together, Alice said. *It's the only way.*

Storm snorted, turning to the wolf pack, who formed a ring around them.

Something moved on a nearby rooftop. Alice glanced up and saw a demon leap back into the shadows. They were cautious, but they would come. They would come for Alice because they needed her gone.

She looked around at her protectors, their ears taut and hackles raised for the fight. They were strong and fast, but against Narlaw they were not enough. She would need time to focus her senses on the demons when they came. She needed more people.

"Defenders!" she cried out. "Defenders, come to me!"

Her voice flew on the wind, vanishing down the narrow, fortified streets.

"Fall back to the square!" she cried.

Now her cry was echoed by others.

"Fall back!"

"Back to the square!"

A door creaked open on the edge of the square

and a woman darted out. It was Elder Byrne, brandishing an ancient, rusty-looking sword. The wolves parted so she could join Alice and Storm within the circle.

"They're everywhere," said the elder, breathless and barely in control of her fear. "We can't defend against this many."

"We have one chance," said Alice. "If we can bring them to us, keep them in one place for long enough, I may be able to banish them. That's all I can think of. It's the only way."

A weary group of defenders emerged from a side street and ran to join them, carrying their lanterns, torches and makeshift weapons. Something bolted across the edge of the square and crashed through a door.

A demon, too quick to see.

They were coming.

The last to join them beneath the tree was Owen. He appeared suddenly from behind an upturned cart and jogged to meet Alice at the centre of this strange band of wolves and villagers.

"I reset the trap," he panted. "But they know to avoid it now."

"They're avoiding me, too," said Alice. "But they will come. They have to."

Owen nodded, peering up at the jagged rooftops of the cottages.

A pair of human forms flitted across with inhuman speed.

"There are more than we thought," said Owen.

Alice nodded. She could feel them drawing near, making ready to attack and to place her in the ghost-sleep as they had Moraine. With both Whisperers gone, these creatures would spread unhindered through the forest, overrunning village after village and ushering more and more of their destructive kind into Meridina. She wished, again, that a battalion of guards, armed to the teeth, would gallop into Catchwood right then and fight the demons off.

But wishing was no use.

A slate slid from a nearby rooftop and shattered on the ground. The Narlaw were coming. Alice closed her eyes, with the band of defenders spread around her, and made ready for her final test.

The first attack was brutal and short. Three Narlaw came together, knocking one man unconscious and badly injuring a grizzled, grey wolf before Alice could turn her Whisperer sense on them. When she managed to, they leaped away like giant insects and then vanished.

The villagers dragged the unconscious man into the centre of the group and propped him up against the tree's vast trunk. He was breathing. He would survive. The injured wolf limped on, ready for the next attack.

He didn't have to wait long.

The Narlaw swarmed from the streets and alleys, furtively at first and then with a brazen confidence, as if they knew Alice had no chance of banishing so many at once. As the group of defenders tensed, preparing to fight, Alice felt the cold, otherworldliness of the demons creep into her mind, their desire for destruction focused on her. Their grey eyes glowed with malignance.

She did her best to stand tall beside Storm, Owen and the others. Even if they were all sent into the ghost-sleep right there, even if the village was taken, then they would have tried; they would have fought against the demons together.

That was something at least.

The Narlaw struck. They came from all angles, closing on the group beneath the swaying boughs of the festival tree. The demons dodged and swerved, preventing Alice from grasping them.

And then she saw Moraine.

Her heart lurched. Of course it was not Moraine, but her likeness. Still, Alice felt suddenly and desperately ill. The true Moraine would be hidden somewhere – hungry, cold and weak. And the hunters much worse.

Beside her Owen cried out for his father, whose face would also be here, twisted into evil. But she knew that Owen understood too. The only way to save their loved ones was to banish these creatures. Right here. Right now.

So Alice closed her eyes and cast her Whisperer

sense across the square.

The Narlaw slipped away from her like phantoms. She tried to embrace them, all at once, then just one at a time, but it was impossible. It took all her effort not to flinch away from the cruelty and destruction that they radiated. With her eyes closed, she witnessed the next attack with her senses. The wolves and villagers shone with fear and determination as they desperately fought the demons off. Their cries seemed distant even though they were only paces away. The demons leaped and struck out at the defenders. The defenders swung their torches, making the demons recoil. A lone Narlaw broke through the circle and Alice retreated, back towards the great tree. Storm and Elder Byrne intercepted the demon and the fight was vicious and swift. Alice tried to hold the Narlaw in her mind, to banish it as she had done the one in Owen's trap. But the creature fled, leaving Storm panting and Elder Byrne near to collapse beside her.

Several of the villagers were lying still on the ground. The Narlaw came in waves, synchronized and distracting. Alice tried with everything she had to hold them to her, to make them a part of her embrace of the village square and everything else within it.

Then a demon presence was on her, dropping down from the festival tree. She opened her eyes and cried out. Storm spun around and came rushing towards them, but the demon was faster. It struck Alice in the jaw and she felt herself leave the ground, then land, all the air rushing from her lungs. The Narlaw stood over her. Alice blinked her vision into focus and gasped into Moraine's face, grey-lit and horribly intense. The Narlaw lowered a hand towards Alice's forehead. Alice tried to scramble back, but the fall had sapped away her energy.

She cast her senses wide. One last try. The Narlaw overshadowed everything. Where was Storm? Where was everyone?

Then there was another presence. Something huge and old.

She knew it somehow.

The Narlaw's cold hand touched her head and

Alice squirmed away. She collided with something, the tree perhaps, she couldn't tell. But there was nowhere left to go.

She waited for the ghost-sleep, still trying desperately to snare this one Narlaw, to hand it to the earth for banishment. But she couldn't hold it. She coiled into herself in absolute fear.

Then came a roar like nothing she had ever heard.

The demon flinched away and Alice opened her eyes. It was the presence, the ancient, hulking presence from Soraya's cave. She saw its thick limbs swing and the Moraine-demon crumpled to the floor. It roared, a jaw full of teeth that glinted in the moonlight.

A bear. It was the first Alice had ever seen, so few were there in the great forest. It reared on to its hind legs, twice the height of a man, and roared into the night. Then it turned on the attacking group of Narlaw, fearless and more powerful than any other beast of the forest. More powerful than a Narlaw, even.

Alice struggled to her feet and suddenly Storm was at her side.

She sent it, Storm said. *Soraya sent her companion.*

For an instant Alice wondered what this might mean for Soraya, but only for an instant. The battle consumed her once again.

The Narlaw had backed away in confusion, pausing their chaotic attack.

Now, Alice whispered.

It had to be now.

She summoned every scrap of energy and concentration, opened herself completely to the chill night air and the rutted earth beneath her feet. This was it. She cast out with her senses. Everything there was became a part of her. The tree, the houses and the wind. The wolves and villagers. The Narlaw and the bear.

The demons fell on the bear all at once and Alice felt the beast's fury as it fought for its life. She brought its fearsome presence close and the Narlaw came with it, their wild movements now contained. For a moment, to the Narlaw, she was forgotten.

And a moment was all she needed.

The Narlaw sickness welled up in her, but the earth was there too, rushing through her mind and body. She felt as tall as the festival tree, as great and powerful as the forest itself. The earth sang in her heart and it burned with fury at the demons in its midst. In a single, obliterating moment the demons were torn away. Alice felt it like a cleansing of her soul. And then the earth trance rushed away and she fell.

She looked up, dazed, into Storm's golden eyes. Storm's muzzle was bleeding and she was panting hard.

You did it, Storm said. *They're gone. All of them.*

Alice smiled, too exhausted to speak. Her head felt empty and weak and the relieved laughter of the villagers came to her as if from a great distance. Where the Narlaw had stood lay only ashy shadows on the earth, stains from their violent departure back to the Darklands. Alice watched as a man she knew as the village butcher rose up slowly from the ghost-sleep he had been thrown into just moments before.

He was bruised and dirty from the fight. Blood had trickled and dried on his face. The whole square was stunned into silence as this tall, white-haired man looked about him at the remains of the demons. He had tears in his eyes.

CHAPTER 14

The infirmary was deathly quiet. Ebony swooped in ahead of Dawn and perched at the foot of Yusuf's bed. The real Yusuf.

Lady Tremaine was already there, flanked by a pair of the king's guards. She turned her icy gaze on Dawn as she entered.

"So you have returned," the warden sneered. "After disobeying the king for a second time I thought you would have fled the city. It would have been a wiser course of action." She turned to the guard at her right side. "Take this girl into custody. But find her a cell in the prison wing this time."

Ebony cawed and spread her wings wide as the guard stepped forwards.

Dawn stood her ground. "You may wish to know

why I arranged this meeting before locking me away," she said.

She met the warden's gaze head-on, battling the exhaustion that she felt inside. The warden said nothing, but the guard paused.

"Captain," Dawn called out. "Would you bring the prisoner, please?"

The warden's eyes narrowed as she looked to the doorway. Valderin entered and behind him came four of his palace guards. The demon that they carried was still locked in its final lunge, limbs outstretched and a monstrous fury on its face – the face of Yusuf.

The warden gasped and her guards drew their swords.

"The Narlaw spy," said Dawn. "This creature sabotaged the viaduct and sank Princess Ona's friend into his present state. Don't fret." She smiled. "I have the demon contained in a protective ward."

Valderin and the guards withdrew, carrying the demon.

"But … I don't…" the warden muttered.

"I am the Palace Whisperer," said Dawn. "It is my task to protect this land from the threat of the Narlaw and that is what I have done. You can order me to the dungeon if you wish, but I shan't be going. I have work to do."

The warden stared, dumbstruck. She did nothing as Dawn turned her back and left.

In the corridor outside Ebony flapped on to Dawn's shoulder. *Satisfying?* she asked.

You could say that, whispered Dawn.

She strode along the infirmary corridor. With one task complete, it was now time to rescue Yusuf from his ghost-sleep.

Seeing the warden squirm had been a welcome consequence of clearing the young man's name, but the victory was tempered with uncertainty. Dawn had a demon to banish, a war council to organize, and somehow she had to find out exactly what the Narlaw were planning. It was no random act, this spy infiltrating the palace. The demon had carried out an act of sabotage, but what Dawn feared most was that it had seen how vulnerable the kingdom was – how ineffectual the king had become and how Princess Ona was utterly unprepared to rule in his place. If the shape-shifter had communicated with others of its kind then they would waste no time in sending their hordes across from the Darklands. They had already attacked in the north. Where would be next? And how long did they have? There were so many questions that Dawn simply could not answer.

Up ahead Valderin and his guards reached their destination, leaving the corridor through a wide doorway. Dawn and Ebony entered behind them. The room was square, with faded white walls and a surgeon's table in the centre.

The guards placed the frozen Narlaw on the table. It lay, stiff and horrifying, in its posture of attack. Dawn stepped up, ready to remove its presence from the kingdom.

This was her first banishment, but she knew she had the power she needed. She had trained long and hard for this day under Esther, the most learned Whisperer of all.

The earth trance came to her as naturally as

sliding into her Whisperer's robe. She closed her eyes for a moment, savouring the rush of feeling that surged up and through her from the living earth.

She reached out and filled the room with her senses. Valderin and his guards stood ready all around her, Ebony behind her on the lintel of the door. And the demon was a nauseous, quaking presence in the centre. Dawn grasped that presence and let the earth's power flow.

It was over in an instant.

Dawn opened her eyes to the white-washed room. She felt dizzy, but intensely alive.

On the surgeon's table there was nothing but an ashy shadow.

Ebony swept down and landed lightly on her shoulder. *It's gone*, she said. *You did it.*

The awe in Ebony's voice was reflected in the stares of Valderin and his guards.

She had done it. For the first time, Dawn felt a sense of true belonging. She was the Palace Whisperer, and ridding the kingdom of Narlaw was what she had been born to do.

CHAPTER 15

The morning sun draped the great forest with soft golden light and the air thrilled with birdsong.

They're back, thought Alice as she trampled through the undergrowth. *The birds are back.*

Storm had raced ahead with the other wolves and Alice had to reach out with her sense to check she had not strayed from their trail. Even such a gentle use of her ability brought a strange, heady feeling. After last night – the battle and the banishing – she felt so exhausted that the slightest exertion threatened to topple her.

She could hear Owen and the other villagers following her through the forest. They had struck out in search of the missing hunters as soon as the Narlaw were banished. Alice walked painfully slowly, often stumbling, catching her boots in the thick weeds and grasses that tangled between the trees. Still, none of the villagers overtook her. She could sense the change in them. Since banishing the Narlaw she was no longer Alice, the twelve-year-old novice from the woods. She was powerful now, someone to fear as well as respect.

In truth, she was afraid of her new-found powers as much as she was proud of them. She had taken a great leap forward but she did not feel quite ready for it; her life had changed – she had changed – and there could be no going back.

A familiar howl brought her back to her surroundings. Storm. She had found something. Despite her exhaustion, Alice found herself running, the desire to find Moraine obliterating everything.

The ground dipped and an uneven wall of rock rose to her right. There were sounds of movement ahead. She saw Storm first, peering back at her in tense anticipation. Then she saw the others.

Some of the villagers lay on their backs, some stood and some sat propped against the trees. All were moving slowly, testing their bodies. Alice recognized some of the hunters, scattered amongst others she didn't know. She heard Owen shout behind her, calling for his father.

An owl hooted.

Alice swung towards the source of the sound.

There was Hazel on a low branch, her head angled in that quizzical, owlish way.

And there, struggling to her knees, was Moraine.

Alice charged into a strong embrace and almost knocked her mentor back to the ground.

Moraine grasped her with weak arms. "My dear," she murmured. "Where have I been?" She looked dazed, puzzled at having woken in the depths of the forest, but she was smiling.

"It's all right," said Alice. "You're back."

Moraine nodded. "Yes," she said. "Yes."

Alice held her tight, and all around them people rose gradually from the ghost-sleep, meeting their loved ones in the brilliant light of a new day.

The morning waned and a mist settled on the forest as they made their way home. Moraine recovered her strength gradually and Alice used the journey to tell her what had happened in the village. She could sense Moraine was disappointed in herself – for failing at the banishment, perhaps, or for doubting Alice and Storm at the beginning. The pain was etched into her weary face alongside the proud smile she turned on Alice. When they reached the burnt part of the forest Moraine let out a gasp. Alice made to steady her against the shock, but seeing the charred trees and her cottage half destroyed by the flames seemed to raise Moraine from her daze. Together, they set about salvaging all they could from the remains of their home.

It was then, with the mist curling through the trees like a cruel imitation of smoke, that Alice saw the raven.

It was perched on a twisting, fire-damaged branch of one of the oaks that stood beside the cottage – a dash of pure black against the mottled forest. Alice lowered the basket she was carrying as she felt the raven's presence reach out to her. Moraine stepped up beside her and stopped, feeling it too.

Images arrived in Alice's mind, an ancient, wild kind of whispering. She saw the shining yellow stone of the capital city of Meridar, the flags flying and a sky racing with cloud and she knew without words that this was a summons.

The images vanished.

Alice watched the raven twitch on the oak branch. Its beak was a great shining curve.

"A war council," Moraine said.

"Yes," said Alice.

Off through the trees there was a thump and clatter of hooves – riders approaching on the north road. The raven tilted its head and swept itself into the sky, huge and black. Alice watched it rise behind the forest canopy, setting the high leaves shaking as it passed. Its presence dimmed and was gone.

"Wait here," said Moraine, creeping cautiously towards the road.

Alice followed and Moraine was about to repeat her command when she paused and nodded. She beckoned Alice to join her, as an equal.

From a safe distance they watched the road. It was just wide enough for a cart to pass and it stretched away for some fifty paces before vanishing in a sharp turn. The thud of hooves grew louder and the first of the riders turned the corner and emerged from the mist.

"The palace guard," Moraine whispered.

There were at least twenty riders, wearing black-plumed helmets and black capes atop burnished armour. Their horses were armoured, too, with thick leather padding down their noses and flanks.

Alice stepped out on to the road beside Moraine. The riders reined their horses in, churning the muddy surface of the road.

"Are you of Catchwood village?" a woman's voice bellowed down from the first horse. The gold edging on her cape marked her out as the leader.

Alice met the woman's steely blue eyes. Those eyes held a look of duty-bound authority, though it was tempered by uncertainty and deep exhaustion.

"We are the Whisperers of that village," Moraine said. "It was we who sent word of the Narlaw."

"Are the demons near?" the guard asked.

Behind her, the rest of the detachment had formed two defensive lines, facing both ways into the dense forest.

"The demons are gone," Moraine said. "There was a battle. My apprentice, Alice, banished them to the Darklands."

The lead guard stared down at Alice with unconcealed surprise. "This little one?" she said.

Alice was about to respond to what felt like condescension when the woman gave an admiring nod.

"Well, it seems you breed your girls tough in the north," she said.

Moraine nodded proudly. She glanced at Alice. "We will be journeying to Meridar," she said. "A council has been called."

The woman gave Moraine a strange look, as if a Whisperer's secret knowledge was something never to be understood.

"Is that so?" said the guard. "Then we will supply you with an escort when our task here is done."

Moraine spoke with the guard, explaining what had happened and what needed to be done, but Alice couldn't concentrate. She glanced back into the trees with a shiver. She could feel Storm, but not see her.

I must leave the forest, she whispered.

Anywhere you go, I will go, said Storm.

Alice's heart swelled with gratitude.

The horses left them by the roadside in a thunderous rush and Alice continued to stare into the trees. She felt Storm there, along with the immense, shifting presence of the forest, and she held on to them both as if they were suddenly more precious than air.

They met at the village gates at dusk – Alice, Moraine, Hazel and Storm. Alice felt her own trepidation mirrored through the companion bond.

The leader of the palace guards came with two of her riders and two spare horses. The rest of the guards would stay in the village as a garrison to help defend against further attack.

A small crowd had gathered to see them off: Owen, Elder Byrne and many of those who had been saved from the ghost-sleep. Alice accepted their thanks with great embarrassment. She hugged Owen awkwardly and then it was time to go on their way.

Alice clambered on to her horse, a docile, tan-coloured animal who was not at all bothered by Storm's presence beside her. Moraine mounted a small, black stallion, with Hazel perched on her shoulder staring imperiously around.

At the head of the column rode a lantern-bearer. The lantern threw orange light across the road, stretching the riders' shadows as they left the village. Alice glanced back to see the village wall and the rooftops vanish from sight. The trees swayed in the evening wind. She smelled the freshness of the leaves, the sweet pine sap and the rich mud. She was leaving the only place she had ever known, away towards strange lands and uncertain times. But Storm was with her, and so she knew that she would be safe.

The lantern swung and the horses' hot breath hissed into the cool evening air. Alice held fast to the reins and let the calm, patient creature carry her away towards the palace and the council of war.

Read on for an extract from
WARNING CRY

the second book in the
Guardians of the Wild *series,*
coming soon!

The sun rose behind Sleeping Rock and, as its rays crested the summit, long shafts of light speared into the savannah – pink, orange, brilliant white. The earth woke, insects buzzed into the air and the acacia trees shifted in the breeze.

Nara stood at the front of the house, her pack, bow and arrows beside her and her water skin hitched to her belt. She would miss this sight. Sleeping Rock would always be home to her, no matter how glad she was to be leaving.

She could hear her father in the kitchen, cleaning up after breakfast. Her mother was tending to the cows, milking them in her quick, orderly way; and Nara's sister, Kali, was busy cleaning out the chicken sheds and collecting eggs to sell at the next market.

All this hard work going on around her felt like a reproach. Nara was a Whisperer, not a farmer.

She had been chosen on the day she was born, when a single white feather landed at the door of her parents' home.

Everybody knew that Whisperers were vital to the kingdom of Meridina, that they were healers and channelers of the earth's power, that they had saved the kingdom from destruction in the past. But still Nara's parents had cursed the arrival of the white feather, along with the raven who had delivered it.

What good was a Whisperer to a farmer's daughter? What use were a Whisperer's skills when only hard work and experience could put food on the table?

Nara was a good Whisperer – she could heal, she could communicate with almost any kind of animal and she could set protective wards that kept predators at bay. But her daily training took her away from the family farm and, at the age of twelve, she still couldn't milk a cow properly, or separate a herd for market or plant maize that would grow in the crumbly red soil of their farmland.

Although her parents never said so, Nara knew

she was a disappointment. It was clear in the way they constantly praised her sister. Kali was devoted to the farm in a way that Nara never could be.

And now the raven had visited their home once again. It had come like a falling shadow, bringing Nara an urgent message from the palace in Meridar. She had closed her eyes and the raven had placed images in her mind. She had seen a strange, dense forest – more green than she had ever imagined. And between the trees she had seen the Narlaw, the shape-shifting demons she had learned so much about in her Whisperer training. In the raven's vision they took the forms of women, men and wolves, and Nara had felt a terrible chill run through her. A hundred years had passed since these demons were last banished to the Darklands. But the raven's message was clear: the Narlaw had returned and Nara, along with all of the Whisperers of Meridina, must journey to the palace for a council of war.

Despite her anxiety, Nara had needed no further convincing to leave. She had packed her things and, one day later, here she was, ready to go.

She watched the morning light creep over the clefts and ridges of Sleeping Rock. Behind her, on the far side of the house, the cattle lowed and snorted in their pens – those great grey cows whose bristly chins Nara had always loved to stroke.

Today she would leave all this behind. Her parents didn't understand the responsibility of a Whisperer – that Nara had been born to protect the wilds, and that the Narlaw were the biggest threat there had ever been.

Nara was determined to show her family who she really was, to go from healer to warrior and banish the demons just like Queen Amina had a hundred years ago. She felt a ripple of fear at the thought. She had learned the theory of banishment from Lucille, her mentor, but to be faced with a real, shape-shifting demon was a different matter all together. They were stronger than three men combined and they could steal your form and drop you into an endless, dreamless sleep at a single touch…

Nara gripped her bow tightly and breathed the cool morning air. She reached out with her Whisperer sense and felt the world around her – the sway of the grass, the bush larks darting overhead. All of this would be gone if the Narlaw were allowed to return. The demons lived only to destroy, feeding on the living parts of the world as a fire feeds on dry timber.

Her journey would span the length of the kingdom, up into the cold and unknown north. To where the ravens roosted and the Darklands threatened from beyond the mountains.

Paws padded lightly on the earth behind her, reminding Nara that she wouldn't be facing these challenges alone. She turned as her leopard companion, Flame, emerged from inside.

Some things are worth rising early for, Flame said.

Her words rang out in Nara's mind and the bond between them grew warm at Flame's approach.

Do you think they have mornings like this in the north? whispered Nara.

Flame squinted into the sunrise and flicked her long, black-tipped tail.

Not like this, she said.

No, said Nara. *Not like this.*

Nara lay her hand on the soft, patterned fur of her companion's back. Flame was slender and proud, the colour of the savannah itself. She could vanish in the shadows of any acacia tree.

A cool day, said Flame, flaring her nostrils.

Nara nodded. There was a thinness to the air, the clouds gathering and shifting.

A good day for a long walk, she said.

Flame looked up at Nara, those sand-coloured eyes regarding her intently.

A long walk we'll take together, Flame said.

The sun had crested the long, barren summit of Sleeping Rock and the savannah was doused in its light – the wide-spaced acacia and date trees, the tufts of red-grass and dropseed.

How cold do you think it is in Meridar? asked Nara.

Colder than we could imagine, said Flame, pacing a circle around Nara.

Well, I'm glad I packed my thickest blanket, said Nara. *Us fur-less creatures have to be careful.*

Perhaps we should go, said Flame. *I don't think there's going to be a big farewell party.*

Who is KRIS HUMPHREY?

We asked Kris some questions about himself and his writing.

What books influenced you when you were writing *A Whisper of Wolves*?

Two books that really influenced how I wrote *A Whisper of Wolves* are *Ghost Hawk* by Susan Cooper and *Wolf Brother* by Michelle Paver. The characters in these books have a deep knowledge and respect for the natural world, much like the Whisperers of Meridina. I also love *First Light* by Rebecca Stead, a book that shows the relationship between an arctic community and their husky dogs. All of these books are mysterious, exciting and beautifully written.

Why did you choose a wolf as the first animal companion?

Actually Storm's character was suggested by my editor, but right away I knew that a wolf was the ideal animal to begin with. Somehow, wolves seem to represent the very essence of wildness – they're reclusive, beautiful and a little bit frightening. Wolves tend to stay well away from humans, but from all the fairy tales we hear as children we know they're out there somewhere in the depths of the woods.

What made you want to become an author?

The books that really got me into reading in the first place were the *Redwall* series by Brian Jacques. They take place in a world where there are no humans, only animals who walk upright and talk and eat huge banquets of delicious-sounding food. It sounds a bit far-fetched, but they are full of imagination and adventure. *The Hobbit* is perhaps my favourite book. I read it when I was about nine years old and then re-read it and re-read it again! It started me dreaming about the stories I could write myself, set in fantastical lands. Although I didn't finish writing any of those stories, I drew lots of maps and had a great time imagining other worlds and exciting adventures.

Where do you write?

Mostly I write at home. I live in an upstairs flat in London and I've got a small desk in the hallway with an old computer that can't connect to the internet. That's vital for me because the internet can be a real distraction when I'm supposed to be writing. I also make sure I've always got a notebook and pen with me. You never know when an idea is going to appear. The great thing about being a writer is you can think about the stories you're writing wherever you are – it's a fantastic excuse to daydream.

If you could be any book character, who would you be?

I'd like to think I'd be Aragorn from *The Lord of the Rings*. He's mysterious, wise and strong. But in reality I'd probably be Frodo's friend Sam. Not a born adventurer, but someone who rises to the challenge!

Finally, if you were a Whisperer, what would your animal companion be?

This is a really tough question because there are so many animals that I love. I'm tempted to choose a big cat, like a jaguar or lynx, but I think I'll go for a black bear. I love their big ears and the way they walk. Also, a bear companion would be great to have by your side in a fight against the Narlaw. I saw some black bears in the wild once. It was scary, but also an incredible privilege. There was a mother bear and a couple of youngsters, one of whom had climbed the trunk of a small tree. I think they were searching for berries to eat, but I didn't stick around long enough to find out.

LOVED
A WHISPER OF WOLVES?

Visit **www.meridina.co.uk** to find out
more about the world of Meridina and
the tradition of the Whisperers

- ❋ **Read extracts from future books**

- ❋ **Find out which animal companion would
  suit you best**

- ❋ **Email the author**

- ❋ **Read in-depth character profiles,
  an author interview and book club
  discussion ideas**

Plus you'll find a range of other activities, including
competitions and details of upcoming events

Follow the conversation online **#wildguardians**

 @stripesbooks

facebook/littletigerpress

 @stripesbooks

ABOUT THE AUTHOR

Kris Humphrey grew up in Plymouth,
where he spent most of his time reading books,
riding around on his bike and daydreaming
about writing a book himself. Since then,
Kris has had more jobs than he cares to think
about. He has been a cinema projectionist, a
bookseller and worked at an animal sanctuary
in the Guatemalan jungle.

A Whisper of Wolves is Kris's first novel.